"WHAT ARE YOU DOING?" DIVINITY YELLED AS JAKE reached into the hot tub.

"Getting you out of here," he said. "You shouldn't be in here this long." He lifted her out, the huge towel wrapped snugly around her damp body. "You could have passed out—"

"Jake Blessing, you're a voyeur. Why, for two cents, I'd punch you—"

Jake's mouth twisted in a grin, but he didn't take his eyes off her. "Having you touch me in any way wouldn't be a punishment. Here, I'll even give you the change!" He lowered her to her feet, then mumbled against her ear. "I was worried about you."

"Thank you," she murmured back, then felt herself begin to melt for real. Jake kissed her ear, her nape, the curve of her cheek. She tried to turn, but he was holding her tight against him.

"Can't help it," Jake said softly. "You're beautiful."

"So are you," she answered dreamily, smiling with eyes closed.

"I thought I was more in control." He leaned back a fraction. "I'm shook to my socks."

"You're not wearing any," she reminded him. "Not much else, either," she noted, gazing with pleasure at the jeans that hugged his lower body.

"You don't know what you're doing to me, Divinity," Jake said, pulling her into his arms.

"Yes, I do," she answered quickly. "I want you. . . ."

# WHAT ARE *LOVESWEPT* ROMANCES?

*They are stories of true romance and touching emotion. We believe those two very important ingredients are constants in our highly sensual and very believable stories in the LOVE-SWEPT line. Our goal is to give you, the reader, stories of consistently high quality that may sometimes make you laugh, sometimes make you cry, but are always fresh and creative and contain many delightful surprises within their pages.*

*Most romance fans read an enormous number of books. Those they truly love, they keep. Others may be traded with friends and soon forgotten. We hope that each LOVESWEPT romance will be a treasure—a "keeper." We will always try to publish*

## LOVE STORIES YOU'LL NEVER FORGET
## BY AUTHORS YOU'LL ALWAYS REMEMBER

*The Editors*

Loveswept ® 782

# DIVINITY BROWN

## HELEN MITTERMEYER

BANTAM BOOKS
NEW YORK · TORONTO · LONDON · SYDNEY · AUCKLAND

DIVINITY BROWN
*A Bantam Book / April 1996*

ISBN 0-553-44522-7

*Published simultaneously in the United States and Canada*

To Rachel, who wants to be
remembered and who will be old
enough to read this book one day

# ONE

Divinity Brown was concentrating, telling herself to focus on the real, not the imagined. Forcing her mind from what she thought she was seeing and back onto the book in front of her, however, took effort. A ghost! She'd seen a ghost!

Ridiculous, she told herself. She was nothing if not a pragmatist. Her work demanded that. Not for her any flights of fancy. She took a deep breath. The apparition had seemed so real, though. Maybe her research had gotten to her. She'd been reading about the old Civil War prison camp in Elmira, New York, when she'd first heard a faint rustling. Glancing up, she'd blinked slowly eight times, looked again, then closed her eyes once more. When she'd opened them, she'd stared at the cloudy figure, although she was thoroughly convinced she was seeing things.

"Hello." Her greeting had sounded hollow in the book-lined room. "Who are you?"

## 2

There had been no answer. Kitty-corner to her right, in front of the Adam's fireplace that sat in the center on the long side of the rectangular room, there was a phantasm. The room seemed to be filling with white smoke. Something was on fire, Divinity thought. That was the only answer for the misty curls. As though to thwart her, the mist took an identifiable shape—a woman.

"Can you talk to me?"

Still no response. She was either looking at Divinity, or just past her, out the window that opened onto the lake. What was there? Water. A terrace. The Christmas crèche that should be taken down. It was past the middle of January. The creature seemed to be admonishing something or someone. Divinity's instinct said it wasn't directed at her. She was an onlooker, a witness of some kind, not the person addressed by the spirit. Though she scanned every corner of the room, she didn't see a corresponding specter. She swallowed hard, making up her mind to walk over to the ghost. At that moment, the manifestation vanished.

No one had told her the house was haunted. Not that a ghost would have stopped her from renting. It just seemed strange it hadn't been mentioned. Most rental properties would boast of such a thing. Of course she hadn't been looking for property attributes; she'd wanted privacy, peace. Her friend Dynasty Jones Burcell had suggested Yokapa County and the house on the bluff called The Arbor.

Divinity looked around the room again. If there

was a connection between The Arbor and the prisoner of war camp at Elmira, she didn't know about it. Of course, she'd just begun her research, so she wasn't that well informed. Maybe the concept of writing about a Civil War prison camp was as flimsy as the phantom. She was going to have to push herself no matter where her research took her. Writing had never been a dream of hers. She'd latched on to it, because she needed to be engrossed in something that had nothing to do with law.

From girlhood she'd wanted to be a lawyer. When adults had chuckled at her childish whimsy, she'd only become more determined. Even after the grueling days of law school she hadn't lost her altruistic approach, her certainty that none could be above the law, that justice would always triumph. Certainly she'd never dreamed of being drummed out of the corps, so to speak. She hadn't been disbarred, but she'd come close.

Forget that! Divinity shoved her mind back to the Civil War. Had there been female prisoners in Elmira Prison Camp? She'd have to look into that. Maybe if she could have asked the cloudy presence . . .

She shook her head. Too crazy. Admittedly she was vulnerable, and had been for many months. Still, she couldn't allow speculation to become fact. Her imagination was working too hard. Too much time brooding on the past was denting her hard-rock attitude toward the world around her.

Her abrupt dismissal from her law firm had had a profound effect. She had to accept and go on, though, or it would put her round the bend. Writing briefs had given her some skill in arranging facts; maybe she could put together a book. At least it was a good excuse to get out of the dwelling places she knew so well, the courtrooms of New York City and Washington, D.C.

The year lease she'd taken on The Arbor should be ample time for her to get her head together. She would concentrate on the present, attempt something she'd had no thought of trying. Did it matter that it had little appeal at the moment? That could come with time, as she learned more, and concentrating on anything but law would bring satisfaction.

A shattering crash followed by an angry yowl brought her to her feet. "What on earth . . . ?" She hotfooted it around the mammoth teak desk and out into the hall. There was more shouting, coming from the kitchen.

She ran down the center corridor and paused in the kitchen doorway, her mouth dropping. "What is going on?"

A tall, broad-shouldered man, busily chewing, turned toward her, then pointed to the other man in the room, Harlan, who had come with the house. A general factotum, he did everything inside and out, and seemed part of the stone mansion.

Harlan was brandishing a meat cleaver at the stranger. "That fool damn near downed your lunch in one chomp—"

The other man shook his head vigorously, still chewing. "Umph-pumph-mumph-ite," he answered.

"What did he say?" Divinity asked, trying not to laugh.

"He says he only had a bite." Harlan glared at the interloper, then gestured to her chicken salad sandwich. A large portion was gone. "Some bite. Ya' took most of it. Damn your hide."

"Not so," the sandwich stealer said, swallowing the last of it.

"The judge shoulda given you life, Jake," Harlan said, grinding his teeth. "Nasty twerp. Always was a pain."

Divinity fought back her mirth as the short, scrawny Harlan, not quite half the size of his adversary, tongue-lashed him.

As though he felt her scrutiny, the man named Jake turned to her, shrugging. "He always gives me a hard time."

"If you don't get out of my kitchen in one minute," Harlan said, "I'll call Dorothy and have you thrown out."

Jake grimaced, shaking his head. "Don't do that, Harlan. I have a good reason for coming here. It's Ephraim's son."

"Isaac?"

Jake nodded.

Harlan wrinkled his nose, narrowed his eyes on Jake, then jerked his head up and down once. "All right. You go in the library. I'll bring decaffeinated coffee in a minute."

"I'll take the high-test," Jake said.

"We don't use it. You'll get what I serve, and no lip."

Jake subsided. "Sounds good."

"We have regular coffee, don't we, Harlan?" Divinity said.

"Yes, Miss Brown, we do. I don't see as how I have to grind nothin' special for him."

"Who is he?" Divinity had an idea he might be her landlord, Jake Blessing. If he was, Harlan was his employee. Unusual relationship. And he was going to use the library. She'd have to gather up her papers.

"He's Junior Blessing," Harlan said. "Your landlord."

"I'm Jake Blessing," Jake said at the same time. "Your landlord."

"Oh. How do you do?"

Jake smiled. "Nice to meet you."

Wow! she thought as the smile transformed him from merely handsome to spectacular. The gloom that had perched on her shoulders so often in the past months seemed to disappear. Her ability to find humor and reason in any situation had been dented after her contretemps with an illustrious judge in D.C. Now all the positive feelings that had been buried so long, were percolating inside, wanting release.

"You look like you're busting to laugh," Jake said.

"I am." And she did. When Harlan smirked and Jake Blessing looked resigned, she laughed harder. Finally she took a breath. "Sorry. I haven't done that in some time."

"Why?"

Blinking, she eyed her landlord. "Ah, not too much has been funny lately."

"I see."

Did he? she wondered.

"Why not laugh anyway?" he went on.

Startled, she blinked at him. "I beg your pardon?"

"Haven't you ever done the imagine-people-in-their-underwear thing?"

"Not for quite a while."

"It works."

"I'll remember that." She eyed the man. He was tall and sleek with an understated musculature.

He was dressed in faded jeans, scuffed boots, and a Carhartt jacket that had seen better days. Harlan had treated him like a boy, yet there was a mastery, a sophisticated aura, a not-quite-hidden take-charge attitude that quivered over him. If he'd played football, he would have been a quarterback, calling the shots, directing the plays. There was a fluidity and economy to his motions as though being in shape came naturally. Surely this couldn't be the person that Dynasty had said some of the folk of Yokapa County thought of as a ne'er-do-well, the county jackass. It didn't fit. Of course, it could all be camouflage. Looks could fool.

She hadn't wanted to be interrupted. Now she was intrigued. What did Jake Blessing want? What had brought him to The Arbor, his family home that he didn't live in, but rented out?

"Not that he ever gave two pins about The Arbor," Harlan said, eerily following her line of thought.

Jake Blessing's expression moved from frown to grin. "Don't believe everything he says."

"I'm still telling Dorothy about this," Harlan said.

The object of his assessment shot him an impatient glance.

"Is she the size of a sumo wrestler?" Divinity asked, wondering how any woman could keep a man like Jake Blessing in line.

Harlan scowled at her question. "Not a bit. Dorothy Lesser Lally—she married Pepper Lally last year—is sweet as honey . . . except she chews his ear off now and then." Harlan jerked his head toward Jake.

"How about once a week," Jake muttered.

Divinity bit back a laugh. "You're the black sheep of the family?"

"Of the county, more like," Harlan interjected, even as Jake's mouth was opening. "Been in trouble since he was in short pants. Burned down a barn once—"

"It was an accident."

" 'Tweren't. You was showin' off for the Skagg girls just before Fourth of July and set off too many rockets. Hit Old Man Weems's farm with one of them in-cen-da-ries. Near took the dairy barn to the ground."

"It was saved."

"By a hair."

Divinity couldn't hold back any longer. Laughter bubbled out of her again. She controlled herself when she caught Jake Blessing's stare. "A distinguished career, I see." She turned away, intending to excuse herself. "I should leave you two alone—"

"I came to see you," Jake said.

That stopped her. "About what?"

"I'd like to talk to you about a friend of mine."

"Isaac?" Her glance skated off Harlan, whose mouth was a tight line. She looked back at Jake.

He nodded. "Have you time?"

"Have you?" Harlan asked, acidly. "I thought Judge Rickey sentenced you to community service—"

"I do that at night—"

"—and that you were supposed to post your hours so Dorothy could keep track."

"I haven't fallen behind, Harlan."

The older man snorted.

Divinity admired Jake Blessing's restraint. He could fire Harlan on the spot. Instead he took what was dished out to him. If he was angered by Harlan, he hid it well. Strange operation, The Arbor. "Well . . . ah, why don't you come along to the library and—"

"You'll get biscuits, jam, and *decaffeinated coffee*, Junior," Harlan interrupted.

Jake shrugged, knowing it wasn't worth arguing with Harlan, and followed Divinity down the hall.

Divinity Brown had knocked him out, like a sledgehammer to the back of the head, when she'd laughed at him and Harlan. He would have done back flips to see that smile again, hear that sonata laugh of hers. She had a great body, though maybe a hair too thin. She was tall, probably not more than five inches shorter than he, and he was six four. He liked that. It also irked him that he found her so attractive. He was there to hire her for her legal expertise, not admire her physical assets. But it was hard not to when she moved like a flowing stream, as though her bones were water, and the tissue and flesh that covered them a fresh cream, not quite butter, just past milk.

Both she and her friend Dynasty had red hair, but where Dynasty had streaks of blond, Divinity Brown's hair was auburn laced with sable, a thick pelt of dark fire. Divinity had been Dynasty's lawyer when Dynasty had run afoul of some serious trouble on Wall Street. Dynasty couldn't say enough about the attorney who'd defended her so ably.

Isaac needed that ability, though it was hard to concentrate on the eighteen-year-old's problems when he couldn't stop staring at Divinity Brown's wonderful curves.

Her hair was so heavy, it should have been string straight. Instead it flared into defiant waves, doing hairpin curves down her back. His nostrils flared as he inhaled her scent. Not perfume, but a sweet soapiness that held its own sensuality. Whoa! Keep the focus, he told himself. Remember Isaac.

He followed her into the library, his gaze going around the familiar room as his mouth tightened. It wasn't that he disliked the room or the house. He'd always been proud of the old homestead. There had been too many bad times, though, that clouded the good things. The endless arguments, his mother's rigid ideas on child rearing, his own stubbornness that kept him pitted against her at every turn. His father's inability to appease his strong-minded wife had frustrated Jake's attempts to be open with either parent, and had often stifled the affection he had for his father.

When his mother had left them shortly after Jake's

fourteenth birthday, and died in an accident not six months later, Jake had been poleaxed with guilt. Not once did his father intimate that it might have been Jake's fault, but Jake hadn't been able to rid himself of the surety that it must have been. In his adult years he'd come to terms with what had happened, realizing that his mother had been totally dissatisfied with her life, not just with her son and husband. He might not have ever liked her, but he could understand and empathize with her pain.

His regret was that he'd never been able to have a relationship with her, or to broach the subject of that failing with his father. Maybe if they'd talked about her, it would have helped. He'd been too damned fearful that last year of his father's life, when his health had been precarious, that he might worsen his father's condition. So they'd talked, but never about Jake's mother.

He inhaled, eyeing the fireplace, the portrait of his grandmother above it, the hundreds of books. There were specters in the room, as there were in the rest of the house. It didn't hurt anymore to ponder them. He just didn't choose to do it all the time, and living away from The Arbor allowed him the freedom to do what he wanted with his life.

"Mr. Blessing?"

He turned to Divinity. "Jake's fine, Ms. Brown." She had a melodious voice. He wondered if she'd ever taken singing lessons.

She held out her hand. "My name's Divinity."

He shook her hand, hiding his surprise at the strong grip. Her fingers were long, the wrists narrow but not weak. She had a fragile air, but he knew she wasn't. He'd watched Dynasty's video of her trial. Divinity Brown was smart and tough. She didn't know the meaning of giving quarter, though she could and would compromise when the odds were weighted on her side. He liked that. That was how he did business. If Isaac was going to be cleared of the charges laid against him, he needed a legal broken field runner who wasn't afraid of the other team. Divinity Brown had the specs.

"I know," he said. "I noticed your name on the lease. My only other tie-in with a divinity was fudge."

"Alienated from the Big One with the capital D?"

He grinned, liking her quickness, feeling a surge of interest that wouldn't be quelled. "Not altogether. We keep in touch."

Her smile was oblique. In a take-charge motion he didn't miss, she walked behind the desk, indicating he take the side chair. She sat, steepling her hands on the desk's teak surface, and waited.

He remained standing, looking out the floor-to-ceiling window behind her. "I see the crèche is still up."

Her eyebrows wedged for a second, then relaxed. "I know it's January, but I hated to see it put away."

He nodded. "It's beautiful. I've been told the statues and crib took almost a year to carve."

"I admire art. Whoever loved teak wood—"

"My great-great-grandfather."

"—enough to have that exquisite piece made had a real artistic flair."

Jake's gaze strayed to the window once more. "I broke the tip of the angel's wing."

"Oh." She sat back in her chair.

Jake understood her professionalism. He'd seen the same sort of quietness overtake his father in the courtroom when a witness was struggling to make a point. He was apt to take a similar course when closing land deals or construction contracts.

"Your father was Judge Jacob Blessing," she said. "County and Supreme Court."

He nodded. "A Blessing has practiced law in this country since the Revolutionary War. I'm the exception." He smiled. "That's why I'm the ne'er-do-well of the family. Didn't follow the prescribed route."

"I see."

Jake had the feeling she did and decided to cut to the chase. "I need to talk to you about a case that could be coming up in the local courts—"

"Mr. Blessing—Jake, I don't think you realize I—"

He leaned forward, his hands on the desk edge, interrupting her. "Please. Let me finish."

She hesitated, then nodded.

"Isaac Meistersaenger is part of a large family of Amish in this area. Fine people. Hardworking."

Divinity nodded. "I've met some of them."

"Both Isaac and his father Ephraim have helped me in my construction company. They're honest, always a hundred and ten percent on the job." He took a pencil from the glass holding an array of them and tapped the eraser on the shiny dark wood surface. "They're family people. Isaac is promised to the Weissman girl.

They're to be married in the spring. They're both eighteen." The tapping stopped. Jake studied the pencil, frowning. "There was a crime in the south corner of the county this past October. A girl by the name of Penny Elgin-Brown was raped, and she named the perpetrator—"

"What name did you say?"

"Penny Elgin-Brown."

"I thought you said that." She nudged the papers in front of her. "I realize that my last name is pretty common, but it's somewhat of a coincidence that it's also the last name of one of the escapees from the Elmira Prison during the Civil War. I've been trying to find out what happened to him."

"A relative?"

She started to shake her head, then paused. "I don't think so, but I don't know. Could be." She eyed the stack of papers. "I needed a distraction. On the way up from New York City I stopped in Elmira and went to the site of the encampment." She lifted some pamphlets. "Interesting."

Jake leaned forward. "I've been there. I would think it would make it intriguing to have the same name as the escapee."

"Yes." Divinity inhaled. And the same as a girl who'd been a victim of a crime. "Sorry. Let's get back to the girl who was raped. You said she named the person who did it . . ."

Jake nodded.

"According to you or the police?"

He smiled wryly at her abrupt question. "It's on the

books. Robby Cranston. Twenty-four, heir apparent to the family geld and property, educated at Cornell, unable, at present, to get into medical school. His father has pushed and shoved at four of them, I understand. Nothing's worked so far. Daddy is still trying."

"You don't like them."

Jake shrugged. "I never had feelings one way or the other. They tried to cozy up to my father, but stopped when he continued to give their brats fines for speeding. The Cranstons are a wealthy family. Their four children have benefited from the best that money could buy. I don't know the three older ones well, but they seem to conform to the family expectations. Robby isn't a conformist."

"Nonconformity isn't a sin."

"I know. I'm a nonconformist. You don't necessarily hurt anyone when you are. Robby crossed the line." Jake threw down the pencil, then picked it up again. "They own a large farm in this county that produces acres of corn, and they also raise beef cattle on another place near the national forest. There's a place in South Carolina, and a yacht harbored in the Keys. They're a very righteous and prominent family who were incensed that their son could be accused of rape. They denied all charges. There was no proof, just Penny's word. She was adamant about it, then stopped pursuing it. The word was out that she'd been paid off because she was pregnant. I didn't know the girl personally, but her friends said she was strong-minded and had been on her own for years. The next information that surfaced was, that at nineteen, not rich, and with few prospects, she'd had a change of heart. She decided to make a case of it and sue Robby, the suspected father."

The long pause had Divinity clearing her throat. "It sounds pretty cut-and-dried—"

"A week ago Tuesday she was found dead, murdered, both her and the baby."

"Good Lord."

"Four days ago the authorities said the blood-stained personal items found near the body belonged to Isaac. It had been quite a battle, the crime scene people said. Penny had fought for her life. Blood was everywhere. Isaac was there, all right. He was the one who found her on Meistersaenger property. He said he tried to help because he thought she was still alive, thought he'd felt a pulse, when he found her, that's why he was covered in blood. He called for help, but when the medics arrived they pronounced her dead. It was bad. She'd been beaten about the head, face, and body, and then strangled. Strangulation was found to be the cause of death, and the ME said she couldn't have been alive when Isaac found her. Unless he himself killed her. He's been accused of the murder and of being the father of the dead baby—"

"DNA can solve—"

"Not if the bodies were stolen from the morgue."

"What?" Divinity came crashing forward in her chair. "Is this true?" She waved her hand. "Of course it is. No one could make up a tale like that." She frowned. "Why haven't I seen it in the papers, or heard something about it on the news?"

"Much of it has been suppressed. The papers talked about the unfortunate death of a young woman—"

"Wait. I do remember something like that." She reached to the side of the desk, riffling through a short stack of newspapers, then laying one open in front of her. "Not even front-page stuff," she murmured.

"Elliot Cranston, Robby's father, owns the newspaper you're reading." Jake leaned forward and snapped a finger on the small column. "The same story was handed out to the city rags. Essentially the incident was buried. It'll rear its ugly head when Isaac is formally charged with the crime. There'll be banner headlines then. Old Man Cranston will make it lurid enough to catch the interest of the tabloids, newspapers, and television. Isaac could be convicted in the eyes of the people of this county before he even comes up for trial."

"It could go something like that." She pressed the top of the desk with both hands. "The bodies haven't been found?"

Jake shook his head. "The feeling is they won't be."

"That puts a different spin on things."

"He didn't do it." Jake grimaced. "The crime doesn't make sense to me or anyone who knows Isaac. He has had nothing to do with any female outside his family except Hedda Weissman. The family wants him cleared, and they can pay for legal help. Their vulnerability lies in dealing with the sophisticated machinations of people far richer than they who have direct lines to the highest levels of the law. Their money won't buy the same protection that political connections to the high courts can."

Divinity said nothing for a few moments. "Harlan told me about your father, that he was honest and respected in this area." At Jake's nod, she continued. "For the son of a judge you seem jaded about the law."

Jake's smile was twisted. "I respect the law to some extent. I think it's corrupted itself by covering up the crooks and charlatans in its ranks. And I think some people get a square deal and some don't. Too many get more perks than true justice, and that same justice is denied to others because they're out of the political curve. I consider that injustice." He noted all the changes in Divinity's expression as he spoke. She could hide her feelings to some extent, but she couldn't quite mask the raw vulnerability.

"I revere the law," she said, "and have always believed in it. I don't disagree with you, though."

"Will you help him?"

"I don't see how I can." She pushed at the papers on her desk. "I came up here for a career change, at least a temporary one. I'm pretty sure this project I've set for myself will absorb a good deal of my time and interest." She spread her hands. "Besides, according to custom, he should request my help—"

"He would if he could. He's in jail."

"He's been arraigned?"

"Later today. He's refused help from legal aid." Jake held up his hand. "Not because he's arbitrary. I think he's scared. I know his family is. Dynasty says you're the best."

"I thought so, too, once," she muttered.

"He needs a fighter." And Divinity would knuckle down for her client, he thought. Her courage was as sexy as her looks.

"Some would tell you I'm all fought out, Jake."

"The way I see it, you're all he's got, Divinity."

Divinity stared at her research material, wanting to get back to it, to ignore what Jake Blessing had said, to forget the law. He'd penetrated a part of her being that she'd been trying to keep under wraps for a while. She needed to back off from confrontation. The battles she wanted to face were those already fought, in the painful past. She needed closure on them. She'd convinced herself that would come when she immersed herself in a nonlegal project.

She studied Jake Blessing. Her nerve endings responded to his obvious sensuality, even while her mind cautioned her to run from the job he'd offered. Strange how she reacted to him. It went beyond his piercing umber gaze, the off-center smile, the sexy, elusive dimple at one corner of his mouth. There was an inner person called Jake Blessing that she itched to know.

"Just tell me you'll consider it," he said.

She sat back in her chair. She had to admit her attorney's antennae were quivering. Surely it had nothing to do with Jake's sexy hands, his long, strong fingers, and wondering what it would feel like to be held by him. The drumming of her jurist's pulse said the case had the catchiness, the mystery, that could push it into big-time excitement. Her woman's blood pressure told her that Jake Blessing would be as perilous to her peace of mind as a barrel ride over Niagara Falls.

Divinity looked down at the desk. She couldn't bring herself to send Jake Blessing away. Perhaps she was a fool. Then again, perhaps she needed to test herself in the arena again. How many Christians had thought they could beat the lions? She might end up being lip-smacking good in a court case that, from what Jake intimated, might be weighted heavily toward the opposition. She'd been chomped on enough.

On the other hand, this whole thing could be a tempest in a teapot. There might be a word or two she could suggest to the lawyer of record, and then be gone. She could see to Isaac's arraignment, call Sol Lechstein and get the name of a good attorney in the area, and be out of there in no time. Did Jake Blessing know it was hard to refuse those brown eyes of his? Of course he did. Hadn't Dynasty mentioned he was a fast man with cards and the ladies?

She looked at him. "I'm sure a lawyer could be found—"

"As I said, he wouldn't accept the court-appointed one. It didn't feel right to him."

"I have a friend who practices in Albany. He knows outstanding attorneys throughout the state."

Jake shrugged. "Isaac might not like them."

He meant himself, Divinity was sure. "Whether he likes it or not, if there's a trial, a lawyer must be chosen. If he won't do it, the court will. He would have been told that."

"I'm not sure what he knows or doesn't know. I

haven't seen him." Jake stared down at the pencil he was thumping on the desk again in discordant rhythm. "His family is worried sick."

Divinity didn't have a good feeling about this. Jake Blessing could be guiding her into a quagmire. "What about the lawyer you generally use?"

Jake shook his head. "The firm started by my father, and carried on by his partners, wants no part of it. Legal aid is still a possibility if we can convince the Meistersaengers it's the right course." He hit the desk with his hand. "Ephraim's pride and fury at such a charge has made him even more bristly than usual. They're blundering at every turn. They refuse to believe Isaac won't be released—"

"If they have enough evidence to charge him with capital murder, he'll probably be held in jail until the trial. If the docket is fairly light, the trial could be soon. That could be an advantage . . ." Her voice trailed off at his level look. She really should tell him no. So what if anger and a sense of futility had contorted his features? This was not her business. She had more on her plate than she could handle. Down the road she would take a case like this. Now was not a good time.

"I'll talk to him." She couldn't believe she'd said that.

Jake's mouth worked into an upward curve. Not a smile, just a touching warmth. "You will?"

Warnings shot through Divinity. Was she letting chemistry dictate her actions? "Just to facilitate things," she answered. "I make no promises beyond that." She hesitated. "Please don't assume I'll carry this further. Chances are I won't."

"You didn't turn me down."

This time his smile was full and genuine, and she felt his appreciation flow over her like a salve. It meant nothing, she told herself. She'd been so battered in the past few months, the merest friendly overture made her vulnerable. That was it. She was as pathetic as a puppy looking for love pats. Ordinarily she wouldn't even notice that drop-dead smile. He'd caught her in a weak moment. She picked up the telephone book. "Is he in the county lockup?" At Jake's nod, she found the number and dialed.

Divinity asked the man who answered a few questions, then was put on hold and left to wonder if she was losing her mind. Listening to a country singer wailing that "whiskey wasn't enough" made her sure she'd soon be longing for the sanity of city practice. Bide your time, her mentor, Sol Lechstein, used to tell her. Study the layout. Stand your ground. She'd be back at it, he'd assured her when she'd told him she'd been fired. The hubbub of big city court work would be hers again. "Yes? Yes, I'm still holding." The smothered sound from the man in front of her pulled her gaze. The limpid innocence wasn't hard to read. "Something funny?"

"I've dealt with Yokapa County Jail a few times."

"According to Harlan, you've been a regular customer." His relaxed attitude didn't change, but she could feel the hardening, a subtle riposte of fury. He'd erected a wall, but who didn't have barriers these days?

She had a few herself. The odd thing was, Jake Blessing had undermined her when his mouth had been full of her chicken salad sandwich. He'd gotten under her skin in a matter of minutes. She must be more down-and-out than she'd figured.

She glanced his way again. He was staring at her. Jake Blessing was going to be trouble. Why should he be irked that she'd rammed his defenses? He'd gotten past hers. The trick would be not to let him know it. For a moment she felt it was too late. Why hadn't she sent him packing the moment she'd seen him in Harlan's kitchen?

There was loud static and clicking in her ear. "Yes, I'm still holding." She raised her eyes to the ceiling. "I should have said it was an emergency."

"Now and then you'd get a quicker response," Jake said. "I wouldn't recommend doing the nine-one-one thing with the county cops, though, not unless you mean it. They can be surly. Not being paid as well as the town boys is a sore spot with them. It doesn't take much to set them off."

"You make it sound as though I'm dealing with loonies, not police."

"Underpaid police."

"Do you think someone's trying to railroad Isaac?"

Her abrupt question snapped his eyebrows toward his nose and brought him out of his slumped position. He stared into her eyes. "Yes."

"Why?"

"Because he's the perfect patsy."

"Hardly evidentiary."

The slight lift of his right shoulder seemed to echo his tone. Succinct. To the point. Quick to shut down again. Lord, she'd been a fool. The last thing she needed was a murder trial with the odds stacked against the client and defense attorney. She had to admit that she was intrigued by the missing corpses. Who wouldn't be? How had someone managed to steal bodies? From the morgue, yet. The arraignment could be interesting.

Forget it, she told herself. She'd give a little advice, maybe a recommendation, and cut out. She was beginning to wish she'd let Harlan throw Jake Blessing out the back door.

"Yes . . . yes. I've been on hold. My name is Divinity Brown, and I'm an attorney . . ." She continued her spiel, losing herself in the legalese that was as familiar to her as breathing.

She pressed the disconnect button, dialed again, and spoke in the same rapid fire way. At the end of the conversation, she slammed down the phone. "I've a couple of appointments. I'd better get to the jail. Where's the county lockup?"

"I'll take you there."

"No need. I'd rather drive my own truck."

Jake rose to his feet. "Fine. You can follow me. Let's go."

# TWO

Jake watched Divinity as they moved through the metal detector and into the jail proper. She seemed unaware of the hubbub around her, the whistles and catcalls that greeted any visitor to the antiquated lockup. The noise escalated to a cacophonous banging when she passed.

Jake told one inmate to shut up. The man riposted with a suggestion that Jake do something to himself that would require acrobatic ingenuity. "They tell me," he said to Divinity, "that the new facility will be finished in three months."

Divinity turned, but didn't pause. "Ah, a grand opening of a jail in spring. Something like a lilac festival."

"Something like that." Jake had barely noticed the clatter when he'd been an overnight resident at the jail a few times. Now he was unaccountably annoyed, his fingers curling into fists. An outstretched hand from one of the cells almost touched Divinity. Jake knocked it away, a satisfied feeling pervading him when the inmate yowled.

"Why bring her this way, Sampson?" he asked the leviathan-sized guard who was escorting them.

"The only way to come until they finish the renovations, Jake." The big guard smiled at Divinity. "You'll like it better when you come back after the first of April, ma'am. We'll be in the new building. It'll be right nice and finished then."

"Why would she want to come here unless she had to?"

Sampson frowned at Jake.

Divinity patted the guard's arm. "How kind of you, Mr. . . ."

"Sampson Dole, ma'am. Everybody calls me Sampson."

"Sampson, I shall certainly try to see the new complex and all its improvements."

"Thank you, ma'am." The big man's smile had a superior air when he trained it on Jake. "Nice to be appreciated."

"Whoopee," Jake muttered.

Divinity bit her lip to keep from laughing, forcing her mind to the issue at hand and off the man behind her. If Jake Blessing was a loser, he didn't come across to her that way. What made him so appealing? He had an annoying way of seeming to see through to her backbone. He was so—so unexpected. Very little seemed to intimidate him, including the goliath of a guard. With his background, he was sure to have clout, but he didn't throw his weight around. Unusual. A tiny houseman could back him into a corner, but he shrugged off a man who must have outweighed him by fifty pounds, and might be able to pound him into the ground. Strange how he could make her laugh and be irritated with him at the same time. She exhaled, feeling the spring that had been coiled so tight inside her loosen. Jake Blessing had a power. It was beyond her to understand what it was, and it made her uneasy. Yet she had also experienced an odd buoyancy since meeting him. Maybe she was coming down with something. It was flu season, after all.

"Open house'll be in May," Sampson said, managing to smile at Divinity and scowl at Jake who had groaned.

"I'll certainly try to be there . . . if I have free time."

"Thank you, Miss Brown."

"It's a date I wouldn't want to miss." Jake's dry comment had Sampson frowning.

They proceeded through another small room, down a hall, then Sampson paused in front of a closed door. He unlocked it and held it for Divinity. "Prisoner'll be out directly." He nodded to the far wall separated from them by a clear, heavy gauge plastic barrier that bisected the room.

"Thank you." Divinity smiled.

"Now you've done it," Jake drawled when the door clanged shut behind them, and she'd seated herself in front of one of the narrow desks. A phone was attached to the wall near her hand. "Sampson'll be calling you every day to come and see the latest slap of paint on the joint."

"You exaggerate."

He grinned. "Maybe."

Before she could say more, a guard and a young man in prison blue entered. The prisoner was escorted to the chair facing Divinity.

Jake, standing behind her, nodded to Isaac.

Isaac fixed his gaze on Jake. "I want to get out of here. I've done nothing wrong." Isaac mouthed the words, and the guard nudged him toward the phone. He repeated them, his eyes sliding toward Divinity.

"I'm Divinity Brown," she said into the phone. "Mr. Blessing wanted me to talk to you about your rights—"

"Are you going to be my lawyer?"

"Well, Isaac, I understand you've turned down legal—"

"If Jake says you're good, you should be my lawyer."

Divinity almost argued with him. Perhaps if she hadn't seen the desperation and fear on his face, she might have made an alternative suggestion. She'd been too hurt herself not to be glaringly aware of someone else's pain. She took a deep breath. "He hasn't exactly hired me to be your lawyer—"

"But I will," Jake interjected.

Isaac's mobile features underwent metamorphoses from surprise, to truculence, to relief, and ending in stiffness. "We can pay," he said, his voice starchy.

"Payment isn't the primary problem at this time.

Getting you released, if possible, comes first. I haven't talked to anyone as yet—"

"Sampson said I was to see the judge this afternoon."

Divinity nodded. "The arraignment. I made a couple of calls before we came. I'll be seeing the district attorney and the judge when I leave here. If there's strong evidence against you, you might have to stay in jail—"

"I didn't do what they said."

Divinity stared at the earnest young man, noting the defiance, as well as the slight quivering of his lower lip. "Then be strong, Isaac. I'll do my best to get you freed."

"Thank you. I don't like it here."

"I don't blame you." On impulse Divinity put the flat of her hand against the plastic in front of her. She waited a long moment, then Isaac put his hand up to hers, a suspicious sheen to his eyes.

She smiled, then dropped her hand to rummage in her bag for a card. "When the police arrested you, did they read or recite to you this information?" She held up the card with the Miranda warning typed on it.

Isaac read it. "I don't recall. Maybe. I think so. There was so much shouting . . ."

"Are you innocent?"

"I am. On my good name and in the name of God, I am."

"All right. I'll talk to you after I've spoken to the district attorney. Don't worry, Isaac." She replaced the phone and gave him a thumbs-up sign.

When they left, Jake asked, "If they have evidence, will they allow you to see it?"

"They'll keep back what they can at this time, but whatever is going to come out in the trial will have to be up front. They can't hide evidence."

"What do you think?"

"Despite his seeming calmness, Isaac is a scared young man. Anyone would be in the same situation." She felt shaky herself. "I think he needs the best defense available."

"That's you."

She shrugged. "It looks that way at the moment."

Jake glanced down at her, feeling an alien tug. Attorney Brown was tough and slick. She knew her business and was comfortable with it. Yet she'd reached out to Isaac as though they were kindred spirits. She'd tried to give him hope. Jake wished he could see beyond the wariness she hugged around herself like a coat. That barrier incited even greater interest in him. He knew what it was to keep secrets, to share part of yourself, not all. That was what vibrated from Divinity Brown. Maybe she was no iceberg with two thirds of herself hidden, but there was a measure of her he'd bet she had shared with few.

In the center of his gut where the little known Jake Blessing resided, was an answering spark of understanding. An empathy had been dredged from him by a woman he'd known only a matter of hours. He sensed she had many, many interesting layers. With it all was a sweetness that sharpened the attraction he'd felt right away. When she'd laughed at him in Harlan's kitchen, when she'd flattened her hand on the Plexiglas screen separating her from Isaac, she'd tugged hard at deeply seated emotions in him.

It had been a long time since he'd been so intrigued by a woman . . . or wanted one for a friend. It took him aback to accept he wanted a woman as a friend and a lover. Divinity Brown was no wispy lady trailing perfume. Her attraction was more like a gut punch. Her cool talent in her field was a turn-on too. What he'd seen of her in their short acquaintance was fascinating.

"What are you smiling about, Jake?"

Could she read his mind? "I was thinking about . . . friends."

"Oh."

"Let's go. We have to get to the outskirts of town where the new courts and offices are. They're finished, except for a few touches. The new lockup is the only facility behind schedule. The judge's office is down the hall from the district attorney's."

When he helped her into her truck, his fingers lingered on her sleeve. Even through her heavy jacket he felt the warmth of her skin. Crazy. It was a damned cold day, and he was overheated. Divinity Brown was getting under his skin.

Driving through the town took mere minutes. Jake kept glancing in his rearview mirror, not questioning the relief and good feeling he had just knowing she was there.

They were one minute early for her appointment with the judge and district attorney.

Jake took a deep breath when the man hanging his

judicial robe on the oak clothes tree looked over his shoulder. Judge Finucane. An old friend of his father's. His glance touched on the man rising to his feet from a chair in front of the judge's desk. Sanford S. Garret. Jake inclined his head. "Judge. Sandy. How's the hunting?"

"Good, Junior." Sandy Garret was medium tall with medium brown hair. His smile was medium cordial. "You should join us sometime. Of course, I guess you're busy with your community service. How's it going?"

Judge Finucane glared at the DA. "No need to bring that up. I know he's keeping to schedule. Duane Rickey told me."

Sandy shrugged and pushed at a folder on the judge's desk with one finger. Then, his smile flashing, he turned to Divinity. "Miss Brown, I presume?" He tipped his head, his attitude edging on patronizing.

Jake stiffened, his eyes narrowing. As though she sensed he was about to say something, Divinity put a hand on his arm and stepped forward.

"Mr. Garret, I presume. How do you do?" She stuck out her hand, just touching his fingers with hers. Then she hauled it back and offered it in a firm shake to the judge. "Judge Finucane. I'm Divinity Brown. I'm representing Isaac Meistersaenger."

"Howdy. I looked over the record after speaking with you, and I think your requests are in order." He frowned, hefting the folder. "You think there's a question about the mirandizing?"

Jake didn't bother to follow the legalese between

the judge and Divinity, though much of it was clear to him. His father, using him as a sounding board for his opinions the many months he'd been ill, had taught him a great deal. Though he still had no interest in practicing, Jake had become pretty conversant with jurisprudence. He might have focused on the conversation if he hadn't been wondering about Sandy's presence. Sure, it was natural for the prosecuting attorney to be there. It didn't make sense that it would be Sandy, though, and not one of the assistant DAs, unless the case would be turning into a media circus. Sanford S. Garret liked being in the public eye. Jake's mouth tightened.

"Something on your mind, Junior?" Sandy asked.

"I was wondering why you thought you had to be here. As I understand it, you have assistants that could handle this."

Sandy's nostrils flared, his smile thinning. "I could ask why you're here. Friend of the perpetrator—"

"Alleged perpetrator," Jake shot back.

Sandy's gaze was cold. "Not that you ever understood the law, except for breaking it."

"Something eating at you, Sandy?" Jake slouched back against the wall.

"Maybe I don't see a lawbreaker like you fitting this picture, Junior." Sandy waved his hand. "We're officers of the court. What are you?"

"In a way I'm an amicus curiae, Sandy."

"Still the arrogant son of the county's top barrister, aren't you, Jake?"

"And you're still the pain in the ass you were when

we were at Crossfield Academy." The antipathy was mutual. They'd never liked each other.

"At least I wanted to be there, Jake. I wasn't bought into the school like Daddy's bad boy, sent there to shape up."

Jake inclined his head. "Take your best shot. As I recall you did just that when we were at Crossfield. How you loved learning about hunting, using guns, bows and arrows, throwing and skinning knives. It was the best part of Crossfield for you, wasn't it, Sandy?"

"Crossfield Academy was a great experience, Junior. The combination of scholarly pursuits and manly sports taught me much. I guess it was there I learned to love weapons. Hunting was considered a gentleman's sport at the academy. And then I went on to Harvard Law School, Junior. You couldn't manage that."

Jake smiled. "Always trying to put people in the place you choose for them, right, Sandy? It didn't work with Ms. Brown, did it? Don't try your games on her. You'll make a fool of yourself."

"Guarding the attorney, Junior?" Sandy inclined his head toward Divinity, who had pulled up a chair next to the judge's and was deep in conversation with him.

"I don't think it's necessary. She seems to know what she's doing. She handled you."

Sandy's face turned red. "Don't get too cocky, Blessing. If I ever get you in my sights, you'll see how well I can take care of things."

"You had me in your sights at Crossfield," Jake said, his voice silky.

"That was an accident, and you know it."

"Do I?" Jake said, but he backed off. It wasn't in Isaac's best interests to antagonize the district attorney. His feathers had been ruffled enough already. Though Jake believed Divinity had handled the introductions well, she might have made an enemy just because she'd arrived in Jake's company. Was that why Sandy had been so bellicose to her? Common courtesy dictated that Sandy should have let Jake introduce her. Instead he'd gone for the jugular, thinking to put her in place before the first hello. She'd foiled him. Jake was caught between amusement and the need to dump Sandy out the window.

Sandy sent Divinity an assessing glance. "So tell me about your new tenant, Junior."

"Why?"

Sandy shrugged. "I always like to know about the opposing team."

"Just another game, Sandy?"

"Life's a game, Junior."

"So it is."

Sandy's smile widened. "And I like to win."

"Don't we all."

"I've worked hard to get where I am, Junior," Sandy continued, as though Jake hadn't spoken. "Getting to be district attorney of this county wasn't a given, as it might have been if you wanted it."

Jake would have liked nothing better than to knock him on his ass. Instead he smiled. Sandy hated surprises. It pleased Jake when his childhood nemesis flushed, his eyes narrowing. "You talk like you came from 'po' folk,' Sandy. Your father and mother had jobs. You didn't suffer any deprivation, except maybe not being where your ego wanted to be."

Sandy's complexion mottled. "Let's face it, Jake, we never got along."

"True. But that shouldn't stand in the way of Isaac getting a fair trial."

"I'm known for my respect for the law." His mouth twisted. "You're not still angry because I called your dog a chicken mutt, are you? After all, he did raid those coops."

"So you said. You were the only one who saw him do it. I didn't believe Bumper would do something like that, so I bloodied your nose."

Sandy smiled. "You *are* still angry. That was back in kindergarten, Junior."

Jake was spared answering when the judge stood.

". . . and that suits me. It'll be done as quickly as possible." Judge Finucane stared down at the folder. "I don't understand how this was mislaid."

"These things happen." Divinity rose to her feet, holding out her hand again. "Thank you." She nodded to Sandy, but said nothing.

Jake said good-bye to the judge, slanted a look at the tight-lipped Sandy, and followed Divinity out the door.

They walked in silence down the corridor of the county complex that wreaked of new paint and varnish.

"Let me buy you a cup of coffee," Jake said.

"I should get—"

"I ate your lunch. I owe you a meal. That wasn't

enough for me anyway since I hadn't had breakfast. If you're not hungry, you can watch me eat."

Divinity was going to argue, then shrugged. "I'll follow you. Don't make it too greasy a spoon."

"You'll love this place. It's called Connie's."

She nodded, then hesitated.

"What?" he asked.

"You don't like the DA. Any reason I should know about it, anything that could color the case against Isaac?"

Jake shrugged. "I don't think so. We've never liked each other. From what I've heard he's a tough lawyer and goes by the book."

"What's Crossfield Academy?"

Jake grinned. "I've always admired a woman's ability to do two things at once. It's an all-around young man's school, teaching everything from the right horse to use for jumping, to handling a weapon." Jake paused. "During a hunting lesson the last year we were there, the over-and-under Sandy was using jumped in his hand at the right moment. If I hadn't hit the ground, he might have put a hole in me."

Divinity's heart squeezed. "You think he did it on purpose?"

"I pummeled him for it and was put on report."

"It wasn't just a one-shot deal with you two, was it?"

Jake chuckled. "Hell, no. I beat him up in kindergarten too."

Divinity laughed. "Remember what I said about the greasy spoon."

"Best food in town."

"Fair enough." She turned away, striding to her truck. Jake flummoxed her. The ne'er-do-well of Yokapa County had gotten to her. Her short marriage had taught her to be wary of men. Hector Deisenroth, a man she'd met when they were undergraduates, had been her first love, and she'd been sure he'd be her last when they'd married. He'd been in medical school at the same time she'd been in law school. Their divergent hours, schedules, heavy study times had pulled them apart.

The blare of a horn and a bellowed, "Look where you're going, lady," brought her out of her reverie. She'd come too close to that car. She waved at the driver, mouthing her apology.

Exhaling hard, she recalled the sad ending of her marriage. They'd gone their separate ways shortly after Hector had finished medical school. She'd already passed the bar for New York State and had accepted an exciting offer from a large firm. Hector had decided to go to Arizona to do specialty work. They'd divorced amicably a year later, but it had left a bad taste in her mouth.

Another horn blaring had her grimacing. "Sorry," she muttered through her windshield.

Failing at something so elemental as marriage had bruised her. Getting into a relationship that had been so obviously wrong had made her question her ability to make a wise choice in that department. Though she'd had relationships with other men over the years, she'd never taken them to the level of living together or making an even stronger commitment. She was damned sure it was no signal flag to happily-ever-after just because a man made her pulse race like Jake Blessing did. That premise had stood her in good stead more than once. It also made her quite sure she could erase Jake Blessing from her mind in a matter of days. Bottom line, he wasn't her type.

Her attorney soul argued that she was building a case against Jake in order to negate her strong, sensual response to him. The woman part of her told the attorney to shut up. She was far beyond the Jake Blessings of the world. When and if she decided on a man, he'd be one of substance; caring, loving, and committed to the world around him. She would not fall for a man when chemistry was the chief component of her attraction to him. At the moment she had time for no one. There was more than enough to fill up her time.

Divinity slapped the wheel. Why was she thinking of the man? Even Harlan didn't have a high opinion of Jake Blessing. Certainly Sanford S. Garret didn't care for him. What was Jake? He was the county weak link . . . who came to the aid of his friends. She'd caught the relief on Isaac's face when he'd seen Jake, how the young man's gaze would skate toward Jake when he seemed unsure of how to answer a query she'd put to him. Of course no one was all bad. Jake had to have attributes. He just wasn't for her. Not that he wanted—Damn! Stop!

She'd been so busy with introspection, she'd gone past where Jake had stopped. She turned onto the street beyond the diner and pulled around a sign asking

HAVE YOU HAD YOUR QUICKIE TODAY? Underneath were listed two luncheon specials. Divinity drove behind the building and parked. Reaching for her purse on the floor, she switched off the ignition. Before she could open her door, it was done for her.

"Hi," Jake said. "Thought you changed your mind."

"No, I—" She was stunned silent when he reached into the vehicle and lifted her to the tarmac. He took the keys from her, locking the door, then turned and pressed them into her hand. "Nice truck. Run well?"

She almost didn't hear him for the buzzing in her ears. "What? Oh. New. So far, so good." He'd lifted her as though she were a bag of corn chips, not a tall woman.

"I thought I heard a slight ping when you braked. Should mention that when you take it in for the five-thousand-mile check."

Divinity nodded, feeling like she was in a daze. "You fix trucks too?"

He shrugged, walking close to her, matching his steps to hers. "Not really. One of my jobs in community service is to go over the sheriff's cars. I'm a helper."

He said it without rancor or pride. Just the facts, ma'am. "Why the community service?"

"Drunk and disorderly. My license was revoked for a month."

"Too much of that is done on the highway. Very dangerous to drive when drunk. The roads are bad enough without—"

"Wasn't on a road," Jake said as he held the door to the warm air lock that kept the January wind from blowing into the diner.

Divinity paused, glancing over her shoulder. "Where were you?"

"I drove my Harley through Danny's bar."

Blinking, she almost caromed into a patron coming out of the diner. "Ah . . . pardon me. I—"

"Hey, Jake! How's it hangin', man?"

"Arbuthnot, how are you? What's new?"

The man looked stunned. He didn't seem to realize he was blocking Divinity's way. "Wha . . . what's the matta' with you, Jake? You've never called me anything but Butch. You hung over or somethin'?"

Jake angled Divinity around the burly man and let the door swing to on Arbuthnot. "Fine. Butch it is . . . only if you remember your mother would loosen your teeth if she heard the way you slang around ladies, Butch."

Butch wrinkled his nose, looking over his shoulder, studying the cars and people in the parking lot. "She isn't here." As if something hit him on the head, he suddenly beamed at Jake. His glance followed Divinity as she made her way down the aisle to the No Smoking section. "That one your newest, Jake? Is that it?"

"Arbuthnot Weems, I might loosen your molars . . . just for fun."

Butch edged around Jake. "Tetchy, ain't ya? See ya, Jake. Make my sorries to the little lady. Don't say nothin' to my ma."

Jake glared as Butch left. He watched as the other

man climbed into his truck and picked up his cellular phone before even starting the engine. Damn fool! He should have called his mother. That would have kept him quiet. Jake looked around and spotted Divinity in one of the back booths, her eyes alight. She was laughing! Grim-faced, he headed toward her.

"Hey, Jake! How's it ha—?"

"Howdy, Joby. I'll see you on the site Wednesday, unless it snows. If it does, call me. We might be able to do something."

"Yeah. Whatever."

Jake ignored the quizzical glances from Joby and his cronies and grinned at the woman behind the serving counter. She was cooking as usual. "Howdy, Connie."

"Hello, Jake. Things okay with Isaac?"

Jake nodded, moving farther down the aisle of booths. He slipped into the one where Divinity sat. "Sorry. I didn't mean to leave you hanging."

"That was asked of you, not me."

Jake couldn't help grinning. The dimples at the corners of her mouth shouldn't be that exciting. Those eyes shouldn't look like topazes because they were full of laughter. That coral-cream skin so taut over the fine bone structure mesmerized him. He could see she was struggling to hold back her mirth, and that aroused the hell out of him. He leaned his elbows on the table. "Just a remark the boys make."

She leaned her own elbows on the table. "I know. Believe it or not I've heard the expression before."

"Oh." He was caught in those beautiful eyes, like

pools he wanted to swim in. "Tough street lady. Right?" When hurt flashed across her face, he reached out and took her hands. "It was a joke. Maybe a poor one, but that's all it was."

She opened her mouth, then shut it again. Looking down at their entwined fingers, she shrugged. "I'm prickly, I guess." Her smile twisted when she looked up again. "Maybe you should steer clear of me, Jake. I'm considered a pariah in some quarters."

"Divinity, I've been in more hot water than three generations of lobsters. I know better than anyone that you can't judge a person from what others say about him or her."

Divinity stared at him, startled by his rough kindness. "I guess you're right."

"Care to tell me?"

Never! She wasn't going to discuss it. "It was the sort of thing that, unfortunately, happens all the time. I've always loved the law. I thought I could solve the problems of the world with it. When I was offered a job as a litigator at Boerman-Dearman, a very prestigious law firm in New York and Washington, I jumped at it."

Jake nodded. "I've heard of them."

Her smile caught on her teeth. "Things rolled along. I was happy, convinced that no one was above the law. One of the pro bono cases I took a couple of years ago involved a young girl who'd run afoul of a well-known judge in Albany. She was accusing him of kidnapping, coercion, attempted extortion. All that good stuff wrapped up in one case. I believed her and went after him, hammer and tong." Divinity sat back, inhaling sharp breaths as silverware was set in front of them. She looked up at Jake again after the waitress left. "How could I lose? I was on the side of truth, justice, and the American way. Of course, I was the twenty-third attorney that the mother of the victim had contacted. None of the others would touch it. I brought the case to trial, and day after day I pounded away with facts, tapes, testimony, and irrefutable evidence."

"And?"

She sighed. "It began small. Phone calls from former classmates, members of my firm, and others. Then there were the face-to-face confrontations, colorful intimations couching threats." She shook her head. "I was so sure my cause was just—"

"Don't be sarcastic about your altruism. It's needed."

She blinked, astounded. Not only was he listening, he was bolstering her. Only Dynasty and Sol had done that. "Thanks. Anyway, I ignored the warnings, convinced of the truth of my case. Despite going up against an awesome war chest and a limitless array of character witnesses, we had some success. The jurist settled out of court, paying an exorbitant fee to my client and all court costs. It was in all the papers."

"I remember reading about it. He should've been jailed."

"Instead my firm bought out my contract, and I became the resident pariah, not able to get a job." She exhaled, pulling back from him. "I talked to Dynasty. She suggested I come up here."

"Good plan." He reached out and took one of her hands again. "It must've been rough."

"It was." Maybe in a day, or a year, she'd understand what had made her open up to him that way.

Jake rubbed his thumb on the back of her hand, ignoring the slight tugs she made to free herself. "I'm not surprised no one would hire you. The people who wouldn't support you would find it too hard to face you, day after day. Keeping you out of the law might salve their consciences, if they have any. Don't let them keep you down."

"That simple?"

"Yeah."

The easy response, the solid advice were unexpected. Her accelerated heartbeat and the blood thundering in her ears were not things she cared to acknowledge. "And how do you suggest I stop the judicial grapevine?"

"Let them see what you are. An honest lawyer. Get into court, muscle your way to a win, use the tools you have as weapons, hitting low, but never quite breaking the skin—"

"Skin past the law, bend it, but don't break it?"

"Lower your eyebrows. You know what I mean. Use their own whips to beat them. Take some hard cases, prove yourself in court. Battling them on their own ground could undermine them."

"They say the best revenge is living well."

"Makes sense to me. Don't bother with the sap

who tried to cut you off at the knees. He'll never know your worth, because he can't look beyond his ego. Judge or not, he was a jerk, and he will be in ten lifetimes. Prove it to yourself only. The rest will follow."

Divinity sat back, shaken. "You're a very lovable guy, Jake Blessing." She felt the blood rushing to her cheeks when he looked stunned. It was dumb. She hadn't planned to say such a thing . . . but she wouldn't call back the words.

The silence stretched over them like a web, dulling the blaring music and loud conversation around them.

A menu was slapped down in front of her, then another at Jake.

Jake released her hand and looked up, frowning at the smirking woman who watched him. "Marcia, our affair could be over if you keep this up."

Divinity blinked, first at Jake, then at the unfazed waitress.

"Breakfast or lunch?" she asked.

"Breakfast."

"Lunch."

Jake and Divinity had answered at the same time.

"I'll have lunch too," Jake said.

Divinity shook her head. "I'll have eggs over hard, and coffee."

He nodded. "I'll have the same with a tall tomato juice—"

"Maybe I'll have juice," Divinity said. "Orange."

"White or whole wheat toast?" the waitress asked.

"Take the Italian bread toasted. It's good," Jake said.

"I'll have raisin," Divinity said, grinning.

The waitress laughed. "She's quicker than you, Jake."

"Thanks, Marcia, I needed to hear that. And I was going to propose today too."

Marcia giggled. "You'll never marry anybody, Jake. Even me."

"You're breaking my heart, Marcia."

A big head came over the booth. "I'm going to break your neck for you, Jake, if you keep comin' on to my wife."

"Gosh, Benjie, I didn't know you were there."

"Ya' did too."

Marcia tapped her husband's cheek. "Behave, Benjie, the lady won't know you're kidding." She smiled at Divinity. "Our son is Jake's godson. Jake saved his life—"

"Did not," Jake muttered.

Marcia rapped him on the head with her pencil. "Don't lie. You climbed down the inside of that silo and brought him out of there." She looked at Divinity, her face solemn. "Buddy, our son, had done it on a dare. The kids saw Jake driving into the farm and told him where Buddy was. They both could'a died." She smacked Jake on the head again, a little harder this time. "He's a true hero. I won't let him deny it."

"Oh." Divinity sat back, looking at the fiery red Jake. He wouldn't look at her, and paid little attention to the remarks Benjie and his friends threw over the back of the booth.

"I'll get your orders," Marcia said, whisking away.

The big head came over the booth again, and Benjie started talking about a construction job.

Divinity studied the two men, her gaze going more often to Jake. The county's ne'er-do-well wasn't just sexy. He had quite a few facets and levels to him. She now knew he was a hero. What else?

# THREE

Divinity was in a blue funk all the way back to The Arbor. She'd been trying to go over in her mind all she'd be wanting and needing from the district attorney, but Jake had been getting in the way. The many faces of Jake Blessing were confusing her. Bad. Good. Sensual. Crazy. Careless. Rebel. Courageous.

She wished he hadn't elected to follow her back to The Arbor. Rather than pull over and say something to him, though, she kept going. When they got there she'd make it plain to him she had things to do, past briefs to check, precedents to peruse, loopholes to find, and gaps in the evidence and police testimony. There was always something. A successful conclusion to a case demanded a thorough preexamination of everything. Not one iota could be missed.

She sighed. She'd been in Yokapa County a matter of days and it had been like a soap opera. A ghost and a bizarre murder case. What next?

Had there been a ghost? Her practical, pragmatic side said no, yet she couldn't shake the belief she'd actually seen an apparition. It was unlike her to accept something so nebulous, so lacking in foundation, yet she couldn't rid herself of the certainty that it had been no figment of her imagination. What would Jake say about the ghost?

No. Forget about Jake for now.

Would he see the ghost? Of course he would—*STOP!*

She needed to concentrate on Isaac Meistersaenger and his case. Her brain and emotions overrode that and fixed on the man behind her. She glanced in the rearview mirror for the fiftieth time. He was right on her tail, driving a cream-colored pickup of indeterminate years that had *4 × 4* slashed on the sides in dirt-caked maroon.

She passed through a small town, then hit the country roads. Miles of fields on either side were covered with brown-beige cornstalks and husks. They gleamed dully through their icy coating. Normally at this time of year they would have been covered with several inches of snow. The shiny, rock-hard frost wasn't nearly as appealing to her. Divinity mourned the lack of snow. She'd counted on skiing this winter, not on meeting Jake Blessing who had elbowed her into a case it would have been wiser for her to pass on. Worse, he seemed bent on ensconcing himself in her thoughts. She wouldn't let him!

Jake picked up his cellular phone when it buzzed, keeping his eyes on Divinity. She drove well, a confident, rhythmic driver. He would have bet anything she could dance. He intended to find out, maybe at the Hunt Club Ball. She'd probably hate—The person on the other end of the line yelled in his ear. "Yeah?"

"Jake, it's Darnell."

Jake froze, his backbone itching, a sure sign he wasn't going to like what was coming next. Darnell Thibaut was one of his father's throwaways. He'd been in and out of the lockup so many times, they couldn't keep track. Jake had kept it from his father when he'd hired Darnell into his construction company. His father had been contemptuous of the day laborer who couldn't hang on to a job, and who had made it a hobby to chug-a-lug his paycheck at Danny's bar. He'd become the night watchman on Jake's construction holding and had done well . . . even with a few nights in jail. He'd fallen by the wayside just this past week. Jake had intended to chew him out about that. "I thought you had three more days."

"Nope. Got out today. Listen, Jake, I talked to Butch. He said you're sweet on the—"

"We're not having this conversation, Darnell." His temper simmered as he contemplated the redneck chatter going on about Divinity.

"All right, Jake. But I've got something important to tell you."

"Where are you?"

"At the site. Mitch let me in. It's the only place I felt safe to call you."

Jake's antenna for trouble quivered. "Get to it."

"I heard talk in the jail about somethin' bein' done to Meistersaenger's place and yours, 'cause you don't tend to your own business like you should. Seems you got some people fired up because you're helping Isaac."

Jake cursed viciously. "Who?"

"Take it easy, Jake. You'll bust my eardrum."

"Go on."

"It seems you made people mad, though I don't know who. I don't even know what they're going to do. But I thought you should know. Ah . . . Jake? Am I working tonight? I could use the money."

"Yeah. Go ahead. If you need cash, you know where it is."

"I don't do that, and you know it," Darnell answered, affronted.

"It's up to you. If you need something, leave an IOU. And, Darnell, no more jail time. Get off the sauce and away from the rowdies. I mean it."

"Right, Jake."

"Thanks for the information."

"Anytime. See you on the site."

"Right." Jake replaced the phone, his mind racing. What the hell was going on? Why the juice on him because he wanted to help Isaac? Isaac's case was the only tail he was pulling in the county. It had to be Elliot Cranston fired up about his boy, Robby. Or maybe it was Robby himself throwing his weight around. He could've been a prime suspect in the murder if Isaac hadn't been arrested. Either way, he'd talk to both Cranstons, and make damn sure they understood he wouldn't be pushed around by them or anybody else.

Divinity turned into the driveway and admired, as she always did, the symmetry of the long, curving entrance to The Arbor. The landscaper had to have loved the place. The combination of juniper, yew, pine, oak, and willow had made the drive a veritable tunnel of beauty. It had to be various shades of brilliant green in the spring and summer; a kaleidoscope of red, orange, lemon, and gold in autumn; and, as it was now, a Daliesque corridor of shiny black and umber in winter. Its many curves hid the house from the road and from neighbors, several hundred feet away on both sides. In the changing seasons the sweeping gardens that stretched away from the house on either side would metamorphose through every hue in the spectrum, as the perennials and annuals preened. Dynasty had described the grounds and their color wheel more than once when she'd been trying to convince Divinity that Yokapa County was just the place to kick back.

Checking that Jake was still there, she couldn't seem to help smiling as he rounded a curve behind her. She swung wide to pull into the barn and turned off the engine. As she got out, inhaling ice-cold air, she admired the circle and squares of light that came from the cupola high above her. The three-story barn was open like an atrium with the center rising to the cupola. Harlan's dwelling was on the top level, an apartment that went around three sides of the rectangle. The five-car parking area on the ground level wasn't full. Her truck, Harlan's truck, and the garden tractor, used for plowing snow and tilling the large truck garden on the grounds, had plenty of room. To one side was a door leading into the tack room, which still held an array of saddles and other riding equipment. Beyond that were the stables. Though no longer in use, they were kept up and in order. On the second floor of the barn was a huge storage area. Harlan had told her it was rarely used. Not even the farmhands who came to The Arbor now and then went up there.

Not waiting for Jake to park his truck, she walked across the turnaround drive into the large area at the back of the house, behind the modern kitchen. Once it had been a summer kitchen. Now it was a huge pantry with a walk-in freezer, and a large fruit cellar in one corner with a sink and countertop that could handle all the accoutrements for canning, and for making jams, jellies, and liqueurs. Divinity liked the spacious area, and that Harlan made good use of it. His jams were mouthwatering. She crossed the large pantry, calling out to the houseman. "Harlan? I had something to eat. I hope you didn't make—"

"He isn't here," Jake said, at her back. He pointed to the bulletin board on the pantry wall. "This is bowling day. One of his cronies probably picked him up."

"Oh."

Jake jammed his hands into his jacket pockets and stared at her.

"What?" she asked.

"Divinity, what would you say if I moved in here? Now, wait . . ." He held up his hand. "I just got a call from a friend of mine. He heard some talk about . . . some trouble. It might be tied to Isaac and his case."

"That's stretching it, isn't it?" She didn't like the hope welling in her, the wishing for his company. It was ludicrous. She didn't have to get all gooey because the guy was good-looking. "There's probably no connection between this talk and the case."

"Maybe, maybe not. It's a big house, though. You can pretend I'm not even here. I just think it might be . . . easier." He pushed his tongue against his cheek. "After all, you might need information about Isaac that I could furnish—"

"The change of address seems a bit drastic." She studied him. "You think there's going to be trouble?" She put her hands on her hips when he didn't answer. "Well, do you?"

"There might be. There's been a lot of talk about this murder. There's some high feeling because the Cranstons are big employers in the area. Robby Cranston was named as the rapist. Some of their workers might think their jobs would be in danger if Isaac is let off and Robby accused of the murder."

"So you think I need protection."

Jake shrugged. "Something like that."

Maybe she'd need guarding from him, Divinity thought. Sharing a house with him would definitely endanger her need to keep him at a distance. He intrigued her, made her feel vulnerable when she wanted to be strong. "You think you should be the one to 'protect' me?"

"Yeah."

"All right. It's your house. But . . ." She hesitated.

"What?"

"You'll have to ask Harlan."

Jake winced. "I know. I think I'll move in first, then deal with him."

Divinity felt buoyant all at once, as though a weight had lifted from her. Don't think of him that way, she told herself. Get your head straight. Focus on the case. "Maybe you could answer some questions now."

He pushed away from the counter. "I could do that."

His intent gaze made her knees weak. She needed to know about Isaac, not about the sexual power Jake threw around like a decathlon contender.

"I want to thank you, too, Divinity."

"For what?"

"Seeing Isaac, giving him hope."

His voice was husky. When had he moved so close? She felt like she was standing in the middle of an energy field. "First . . ." Her voice trailed off as she gazed at him.

"Yes?" His hand lifted. So did hers.

For a wisp of time their fingertips touched.

She watched his Adam's apple move up and down as though he'd swallowed a rock. He bent his head to hers, and she felt his warmth before he even touched her. As she watched his descending mouth, her pragmatic side wanted to tell him to bug off; but the part of her that was all woman begged him to hurry.

It took forever for them to connect. It took a split second.

He sighed into her mouth, his tongue touching hers. The kiss lasted an eternity. It was over in a moment.

Pulling back, she looked up at him. "Bedroom privileges don't go with the lease."

"Right." He urged her back into his arms, his hands sliding over her as hers did their own searching.

His lips were soft as they scored over her mouth and face, down her neck and back to her mouth.

The exploration was the most erotic thing she could ever imagine. She couldn't stop her hands from pressing, seeking. His body was beautiful . . . and hard. Lord! She'd lost her mind. She clutched him, her tongue laving his, wanting more.

He broke the contact first. She blinked up at him.

"I'd—I'd better leave," he said.

She nodded.

"I'll be back in an hour." He kissed her cheek. "You're too beautiful, Divinity," he said, and left.

"So are you," she whispered.

After he'd left, the house seemed cavernous, as though all the rooms had emptied of furniture and ballooned in size. The silence had an echoing resonance that reminded her of a museum at closing time. Maybe she'd notice the clanging of armor next.

Fantasies were foolish, and Jake Blessing had made

her fanciful. He'd certainly knocked the chocks out from under her firm resolution to stay away from any romantic involvement. Stop! She was a hard-rock realist, not some pie-in-the-sky dreamer. She could handle her life and Jake Blessing. He was intriguing. So what? She could handle that. She left the kitchen, going down the hallway to the library.

Walking into the gloomy room, she put her hand on the light switch, then stopped. The apparition! Only a few feet away. Right where she'd been before and this time Divinity was sure it was a woman. Though the clothing was cloudy and unidentifiable, the features were clear, as were the hand gestures.

"What do you want?" she asked. "Why have you appeared now, to me, and not to Harlan or Jake?"

No answer, but the ghost did seem to angle more toward her.

Divinity gasped at the sadness on her face. "What is it? Is it because I'm researching the past? I don't want to hurt anyone. Please believe that. If only you'd—"

She was gone!

Divinity inhaled, feeling shaken. She had seen a ghost. Now, she'd swear to it. Why? Going over to the desk, she stared down at her research, still dwelling on what she'd seen. Blinking, she looked closer at the book on her desk. She must have absentmindedly turned the page when she was talking to Jake. The book was still open to the section on the Civil War, but not about the Elmira Prison Camp. Instead, it was about John Wilkes Booth and Mrs. Surratt. Mrs. Surratt's name was underlined. She wondered why, then she recalled the many research books she'd used in college and law school. Often they'd been marked and underlined. John Wilkes Booth and Mrs. Surratt. Was there some sort of connection to Elmira Prison Camp? If so, what?

Turning back to the section she'd been reading, she leaned over the desk, chin in hand, wondering if she shouldn't just put aside her research for the time being. She had plenty of digging to do for Isaac's case.

Not even the ghost kept Jake from her thoughts. Soon he'd return and he'd be staying. They'd see each other morning, noon, and night. No, not that much. He had a construction company to run. He built things. Just the thought of watching him clamber around a half-finished building wearing worn jeans and a tool belt around his hips made her feel hot and moist. Maybe she really was coming down with the flu. That could account for the weakness she felt when he looked at her. He had the sexiest mouth. What would it be like to see him across a breakfast table every morning? Donuts and sexy kisses? Lord! They could discuss . . . buildings over lunch. She was getting delirious. Maybe she needed vitamins. A and B, perhaps all the way to Z? Or perhaps she was going through a stage. A vulnerable-to-sensual-men-with-great-pecs-who-could-kiss-in-the-gold-medal-class stage.

Why had she agreed so quickly to his moving in? It was insanity. It would be an invasion, not a visitation.

He wasn't there yet and already he was filling her mind.

Forget him. She had to find out what sort of autopsy had been done on Penny Elgin-Brown before her body was stolen. Surely the county had a crime lab. When would Jake be back?

# FOUR

Jake took the stairs down two at a time, intent on sharing his breakfast with Divinity. He'd never been one for breakfast, but in the week he'd been living at The Arbor with her, he'd become addicted to that morning meal. Or rather, he'd become addicted to seeing her first thing in the morning—and any other time of day. The more time he spent with Divinity, the more certain he was that his first impression of her was on the mark. This was a woman he wanted in his life for a very long time, as a friend and as a lover.

Unfortunately, Divinity apparently didn't feel the same way. A week ago, when he'd kissed her in the pantry, he'd been sure that the sparks were flying in both directions. Yet since then, although she was always friendly with him, she'd avoided being alone with him. It was as though she'd erected a glass barrier, and he couldn't figure out why.

He started down the main hall toward the kitchen,

but paused when he reached the library. The door was open, and he heard a faint sound from within. Peeking inside, he saw Divinity standing on a wooden stepladder, reaching for one of his father's law books on a top shelf.

"Careful," he said, walking into the room. "I wouldn't want the best attorney this side of the Mississippi breaking a leg because of a five-pound law book."

She hefted the tome and climbed down the ladder. "Thanks for your concern," she said, dropping the book on the desk with a loud thud. "Your father has the best law library I've ever seen, outside of a university."

"It was his passion," Jake said, walking farther into the room. He would much rather be talking about another kind of passion with Divinity, but he knew he shouldn't push it. He'd have to wait for the lady to come to him. But perhaps a little suggestive teasing wouldn't be out of line.

"Ready for breakfast?" he asked, stopping within half a foot of her, definitely within her personal space.

She stepped away, around to the side of the desk. "I already ate," she said, not looking at him. She opened the book she'd just taken from the shelf and stared down at the table of contents.

Not deterred, Jake followed her. "Well, then, would you mind if I brought my coffee in here? I've got some thoughts about Isaac's case that I'd like to discuss with you before I leave for the site this morning."

She moved away again, concentrating on the book,

swiveling it on the desk so she could keep reading it. "Maybe we can talk tonight. I'm really into finding a certain precedent here."

Jake flattened his hand on the book and leaned over, putting his face right up to hers. "I'm not sure I can wait that long, Divinity."

She finally looked at him, and he was pleased to see both irritation and awareness of his closeness in her eyes. At least he was getting a reaction from her. "Jake, I really think—"

"I really think," he interrupted, his voice low, "that my day will be ruined if I don't kiss you right now."

She opened her mouth to respond, but nothing came out. Nor did she move away. Not one to ignore an advantage, Jake stepped around the desk, grasped her by the upper arms, and kissed her.

Kissing her was an explosion of light, and sparks cascaded through his body, firing his desire for her. He slanted his mouth over hers, parting her lips, finding her tongue. Kissing Divinity wasn't like anything he'd ever experienced, and he wanted more. Aflame with need, he slipped his arms around her.

Her body seemed to flow against his as her own arms rose and twined around his neck. She was kissing him back, strengthening his already powerful arousal. His hand slid down her back, pressing her hips against his.

Suddenly, she was gone. She'd wrenched herself from his arms and put the width of the desk between them within seconds. She stood there, breathing heavily, her lips moist and red, her eyes still faintly glazed with arousal. That arousal faded swiftly, though, as her expression became cool and distant, and he felt like he was facing an opposing attorney in a courtroom.

"I've tried to keep things on a friendly basis between us," she said, "but you apparently haven't gotten the message."

"Apparently not," he said, leaning against the desk, unfazed by her clipped tone. "Why don't you spell it out for me?"

"I'm not interested. I'm not interested in either a brief fling with you or in a longer affair. I don't do one-night stands, or one-week stands, or whatever it might be with you, and now is not the time for me to start something more . . . committed."

Jake noted that she didn't say that he was the wrong man, just that now was the wrong time. "And why can't you start something more . . . committed?"

She threw her hands up in exasperation, then gestured to the desk, which was filled with papers, notebooks, and law books. "I'm currently defending a man charged with murder—a man who is your friend and whom you begged me to represent. I have to give all of my attention to this case, not be distracted by . . . by . . ."

"Sexual pleasure?" he suggested. "Erotic ecstasy?"

"By a man whose ego is too big for his britches!" she snapped.

He laughed. "All right, all right. I get the message." He pushed away from the desk and walked to the door. "No more kisses, counselor. At least . . ."

He glanced back at her and winked. "Not until you realize you want them as much as I do."

He closed the door, thoroughly pleased with her shocked expression.

The first day of the probable cause hearing dawned overcast and cold. The weather had flexed its muscles in early February and brought a thrust of frigidity that an unusually timid winter had almost bypassed. Huge grayish snow clouds threatened, drooping low, sometimes masking the sun. Snow was coming! Skiers cheered. Road crews groaned.

To Divinity the hearing was a jousting match, nothing more. Sandy Garret was skillful in maneuvering hearsay into fact. Since she'd learned her legal body blocking in the courts of Albany, New York City, and Washington, D.C., she was prepared for most of it. She effectively buried introduction of some of the prosecution's so-called evidence, such as Isaac's presence at the girl's death, a foregone conclusion of guilt.

As she listened to the DA, the picture began to change for Divinity. Convinced of her client's innocence, she had an uncanny certainty that there was more to the case than the circumstances presented. The case against Isaac had a bad feeling that raised her hackles. She was too aware of the shenanigans that some jurists practiced, not to know that people could be railroaded. Her hunch strengthened that it was going to be attempted with Isaac. She sensed a definite antipathy toward him. Was it because he was Amish?

Or was there a need to get the case adjudicated as speedily as possible?

The first day of the hearing finally ended. Divinity was almost the last to leave the courtroom. When she looked up from replacing her papers back in her briefcase; Elliot and Robby Cranston were in front of her. "Yes?" she said. "I'm in rather a hurry if you don't mind—"

"Miss Brown, you've taken up a lost cause. Isaac Meistersaenger is guilty and should be locked up."

"I don't believe we've met," she said.

"I'm Elliot Cranston and this is my son, Robby."

"How do you do." She smiled. "I don't intend to discuss this case with you. It could be prejudicial, even illegal. So, if you'll excuse m—"

"If you're smart, you'll cop a plea, Miss Brown."

"Stuff it," Divinity muttered, swinging around the duo and heading out to the main corridor. If they wanted a fight, she'd give it to them. The Cranstons and their money weren't going to stop her. They'd get every trick and talent she had, but they damn well weren't going to get Isaac.

She'd felt Isaac's pain and fear during the hearing. Time and again she'd put her hand on his arm to keep him from crying out. Rage and fear had been in every line of his body.

"Miss Brown! Wait."

"Sorry. No comment." She tried to storm through the swarm of local reporters that closed around her in the hall, giving them noncommittal responses. Let them feed whatever they chose to the national media. As the trial progressed she would do her own doling out of facts.

"Does Meistersaenger have a chance?"

"Of course." Like an uneven parade they trailed her along the long corridor leading to the elevators. She punched the down button and struggled with the urge to tap her foot while she waited. She knew from experience that any overt sign of nervousness or impatience could and would be interpreted a dozen different ways. She stayed still, schooling her features into polite dismissal. Questions rained over her like shrapnel, biting, cutting, snapping at truth and falsehood, anything to bring her blood to a boil. If they thought to puncture her silence that way, they didn't know their woman. Divinity stalked around a persistent photographer who had stepped in front of her, and faced the shiny metal elevator doors.

"Is Isaac Meistersaenger's guilt a foregone conclusion?"

"Does he have a chance?"

"Isn't it true he violated her after death? Is necrophilia acceptable to you?"

"Have you ever handled capital murder before?"

"Take this."

Divinity looked down at the envelope thrust into her hand as the elevator arrived. She stepped in and the doors shut. She was alone. She opened the missive.

*She wasn't the first*

Stunned for a moment, she looked up, jabbing at the elevator console. She needed to go back up, find the person who had pushed the note into her hand. The voice. Had it been young or old? Male or female? Defeated in her wish to return, she rode the elevator to the first floor. She was still staring at the note when she exited. She felt Jake's presence before he spoke.

"Why did Linnie give you that?"

Divinity looked up at him, blinking. "You saw who gave me this? You were upstairs?"

He nodded. "I was able to get away from the site early and got here just as everyone was leaving the courtroom. I saw how the reporters were badgering you and thought it would be better if I kept my distance. I took the stairs down."

"Tell me about Linnie."

"She used to live in the area. Moved to Geneva a couple years ago." He eyed the paper, and she held it out to him.

"What's her full name?"

"Linda Glenhurst. Everyone's always called her Linnie. Her uncle worked for me until he died." He looked around the large anteroom. "Let's get out of here. You're probably hungry."

"What?" Her mind was on his strong hand as he cupped it around hers, definitely not on food. "I can't go to lunch now. I want to see—"

"We'll take care of that too."

"Oh. Shall I follow you?"

"No need. I'll ride with you. Darnell took my truck."

"Are you sure about this? I want to talk to Linnie Glenhurst as soon as I can. I need to know why she gave me the note, and exactly what she meant."

"That's where we're going now."

Relieved, she nodded. "Good. How about your work?"

"It's fine. Darnell, Benjie, and Butch are handling things."

"Oh." She was almost at a trot as she accompanied him across the parking lot, head ducked to keep most of the freezing air off her face. Jake was in front of her, blocking the worst of the harsh winter wind.

He opened the driver door. Divinity thought he was going to drive her truck until he gestured she get behind the wheel. "Climb in, Divinity. It's forty-below windchill out here."

Her heart went into a nosedive as he put his hands around her waist and lifted her up onto the seat. Since the day he had kissed her in the library and she had told him she wasn't interested, he'd kept his distance. More or less. Although his touches were never sexual, he seemed to find a lot of reasons to touch her. Helping her on and off with her coat, pouring her coffee and handing her the mug so that his fingers grazed hers, things like that. And every one of those apparently innocent touches fired her blood in a way that other men's most passionate kisses never had.

Jake climbed in the passenger side and blew on his hands. "Got a bite to it." He grinned when she laughed. "It has a nice sound . . . your laugh, that is."

"Thanks." Her mind churned with Jake Blessing

and a multitude of facts. He'd put her in a maelstrom. He was too damned sexy. She tried to rev up at least indifference to Yokapa County's ne'er-do-well. What surfaced was something else. She liked Jake . . . more than a little. He didn't make assumptions about anybody, treating all people on an even scale.

"What's on your mind?" he asked.

"Ah, the trial."

"And more. Want to talk about it?"

"There are too many holes in this case. The trial is sooner than I'd wished." She thumped the steering wheel. "I need a starting point."

"Linnie."

She nodded, slicing a glance at him as she changed gears and drove from the parking lot. "For a ne'er-do-well, you're smart and pretty virtuous."

He laughed. "Virtuous is not a word that's been applied to me."

"I see. So if I said you're more Galahad than do-nothing, you'd think I was off the mark."

His continued silence, even when she was no more than a coat of paint from an eighteen-wheeler as she veered around a senior citizen doing ten miles an hour under the speed limit, elicited another glance. "I've shocked you?" she asked.

"Maybe. I thought you'd want to talk about the case."

"I do. You keep getting in the way."

His chuckle was deep and sexy. "You're plainspoken. I like that."

"Thank you."

"Are you worried about the case?"

"It's bothersome, I'll admit. I'm more worried about Isaac. He's getting downhearted. I don't like that."

"He'll be fine. So will you."

"Right. Let's change the subject." She took a deep breath and jumped. "Have you ever seen a ghost at The Arbor?"

Jake had been snapping the anonymous note in his hand. He stopped, slanting a look at her. "I've heard tales about them since I was a kid. Why? Have you seen one?"

"Yes."

"What?" He straightened in his seat, turning her way. "When? What was this ghost like? Did he talk to you?"

"The day you arrived to tell me about Isaac. It wasn't a he. I couldn't make out what she was saying, but she seemed to be looking out toward the lake."

Jake was silent.

"You don't believe me."

"Wait a minute, Divinity. Don't take fences. I didn't say that. I'm just a little surprised. Who wouldn't be?"

"Same thing."

He sank back in the bucket seat, looking out at the many marinas and tackle places along the Seneca River as they headed west on Route 5 and 20. "Let me say this. From boyhood I've heard tales about the Blessing ghost. I always assumed it was a man, maybe the Blessing who fought with George Washington."

72

"Who else could it be?"

"Some said it was Levi Blessing who disappeared at the Battle of Gettysburg. His remains were never found, so he haunts the place."

"Makes sense."

"Maybe. Since I've never had a visitation, I outgrew the stories and the hope I'd meet my ancestor." He shifted behind his seat belt. "I don't disbelieve you. I'm just not into it." He turned toward her, his one hand going out to her hair, touching it, then pulling back as though he'd just realized he'd done it. "You wouldn't lie. You're an honorable person."

The flat statement almost sent her off the road. She gripped the wheel tighter. "Thank you."

"Don't let the road rovers shake you up. Some think they own the highway."

"I don't argue with trucks larger than mine."

"Smart plan." He chuckled. "You're a good driver."

"Why is that funny?" She was being defensive. She couldn't help it.

"I was wondering what you'd say to one of them face-to-face."

"Are we talking about the ghost or the truck driver?"

He sent her a curious glance at her sharp tone. "Ghost."

"Sorry. I didn't mean to be testy." She exhaled. "The last several weeks have been bummers and—"

His laughter interrupted her.

"That's funny to you?"

"Yeah, I guess. Since meeting you I've been enjoying life more. Not that I'm taking Isaac's case lightly. I'm not. But you've managed to bring some winter sunshine to Yokapa County. I like that."

"Ah, thanks." She grimaced. "I keep doing that, thanking you. That's got to stop."

His laughter loosened some of the tension inside her, coaxing out her own laughter. Like breathing clean air, it energized her. "I mean it," she said.

"I don't mind."

"Are you too good to be true, Jake?" When he gulped, she chuckled. "I guess that was blunt."

"Nice, though."

"I'm just not used to Yokapa County people yet."

"We have our ways. So do you."

She glanced at him. "Oh?"

"You're an unusual person, Divinity, and I'd like to be your friend."

Taken aback, she shook her head, fastening her gaze on the highway as it widened to four lanes. They were entering the outskirts of Geneva. "Where to?"

"Keep going. We don't take the first turn." Jake leaned forward. "The lake's pretty steamed up."

Divinity glanced left. "That's Seneca Lake, isn't it?"

"Yes. The water temperature is probably around forty. Since the air temperature is seven below zero, we're getting steam."

She smiled, unbending. "Not as warm as a hot tub."

"No. But if you like that sort of thing, we have one at The Arbor."

"A hot tub?"

"I had it put in for my father. Short stretches in it alleviated some of his pain."

"It was hard to lose him."

"Yes. We'd gotten closer the months he was ill." Jake pointed. "Turn here."

Divinity followed his directions to Exchange Street and the corner coffee shop. "I think I'd rather find Linnie Glenhurst than have—"

"That's what we're going to do." He grinned at her puzzlement. "Bernie, who does the cooking at the café, knows everybody and what everyone's doing. He's made it his life's work."

Divinity chuckled. "I'm amazed at the way information travels in this area."

"Faster than an eagle flies."

She parked the truck and buttoned her coat. Jake went around to the driver's side and opened her door.

"Hi." He lifted her out from behind the wheel.

"You're always doing that."

"I know." He looked both ways, then took Divinity's arm and they loped across four lanes of traffic, dodging cars slowing for the light. They had to climb a snow pile to get to the sidewalk. When Divinity slipped, Jake slid his arm around her, keeping her close to him. She shivered.

"Are you all right, Divinity?"

She nodded. She could feel his warmth through her

coat. Fighting an urge to lean against his chest and close her eyes, she strode ahead, aiming for the door.

Jake reached around her to open it. The wind all but tore it from his hand. He edged her inside. "Damn windchill. Once it settles, the skiing will be great." He smiled down at her. "I'll take you over to Greek Peak."

She didn't answer, hoping he'd think the cold had frosted her tongue. Her insides were doing the tango. Jake Blessing had a blistering smile. "Sounds great," she managed to say.

He reached around her and opened the inner door, and she inhaled the welcome pungency of coffee and the fresh bread lining the counters. "Mmmm. That smells wonderful. Coffee and some of that bread would be good."

Jake chuckled. "They make the raisin bread every day, and it's gone before five."

They sat at a round table near the window fronting on the sidewalk.

Divinity scrutinized every booth, each person eating at the food bar in front of the grill. "Is she here?"

"No, but I'll ask Bernie if she ever comes in. If not, we'll go to the antique store where she works." He ambled down the long serving bar, getting the attention of someone at the steam table.

Divinity studied him, noting the number of people who spoke to him, the quick smiles. He greeted everyone, but didn't pause on his return to her.

He straddled his chair. "I ordered coffee, toast, and eggs. Bernie said Linnie should be in anytime now. She comes in every day around this time to pick up coffee and snacks for everyone at the antique store. They've already called in their order, so she should be here soon."

"This could be nothing or the break I need," Divinity said.

"It'll be what you want. I'm sure of it."

She couldn't fathom why that reassured her, but it did.

The food came, and she all but salivated. "It looks wonderful."

Jake sat back with his coffee. "Tell me more about our ghost."

Divinity dabbed at her mouth. The good food was helping to relax her. "I can't describe her really, except I know she's female and not too old." She paused as the door opened.

Jake looked up, then nodded to her. He slipped out of his chair and followed the woman who had entered the coffee shop.

"Linnie."

She turned, her smile warm. "Jake. Hi. What brings you to Geneva?"

He took hold of her arm. "I brought Isaac's lawyer here." She whitened. "Easy. It's not a problem, I promise. I need to have the note explained, Lin. So does Divinity. We need all the help we can get. Sit with us for a minute."

She bit her lip, glancing around the shop. "I can't, Jake. I took the morning off to go to the hearing. I have to get to work."

"Okay. Don't get upset. Let me handle it." He

looked over at Bernie. "Hold Linnie's order for her. And put it on my bill," he added, throwing some money on the counter. "I need to use the phone."

Bernie nodded. "Pay phone's at the end of the counter, Jake."

"Give me the number of the store, Linnie," he said as they walked to the phone.

Jake dialed, talked into the receiver, and smiled at the answer. He cradled the phone. "Sam says take all the time you want. You spelled him for two weeks when his wife had her baby."

Linnie almost smiled, but trepidation settled over her when she took a chair adjacent to Divinity. "I'm the one who gave you the note."

Divinity nodded. "Tell me what you meant."

Linnie glanced around the café, seeming to breathe easier when she looked back at Divinity. "My roommate . . . Janis Wismer." She folded and refolded her hands, squeezing her fingers as though she was trying to hold on to something . . . or let it go. "They said she killed herself. She didn't. I knew her real well. She wasn't down or depressed. She and I talked about everything. She wasn't pregnant either. That's the rumor that went around, that she killed herself because she was going to have a baby and was afraid to get an abortion. That wasn't true, but she was involved with that crowd, and I think they started the talk—"

"Crowd?"

Linnie itched around in her chair. "You know, that bunch that hangs around the islands in the river. They do all the heavy drinking . . . and drugs and stuff."

Divinity eyed Jake. He shook his head.

Linnie took a deep breath. "I wouldn't go along with their stuff because I never trusted them, but I couldn't convince Janis they were no good. She thought it was glamorous, that they were fun . . . just like the guys in the soap operas, she said. Baloney. They're all losers, and that's what I told her." Linnie grimaced. "Don't get the wrong idea about Janis. She was great. She and I went to school together, and I knew she didn't do drugs. That's why when they found her and said she'd OD'd, I knew it wasn't true. She was a little silly about partying, thought it couldn't hurt . . ." Linnie's voice trailed off. "She was so cute. She just didn't see that bunch for what they—"

"What is it, Linnie?" Divinity asked when the other woman stopped abruptly. "Have you remembered something?" She didn't raise her voice, though her heart pounded.

"Not really. I might be mistaken. Janis never mentioned names, but I had the feeling that not all the people in that group were river rats, that maybe some of them had money." She made a face, shrugging. "She might've meant Robby Cranston. He has money."

She took a deep breath. "I'm not sure I have this right, but I think she told me that a girl in that group died . . . before her, I mean." She wrinkled her nose. "But I think it was an auto accident."

"What was her name?" Jake asked.

"Don't have one. I'd like to help you, Jake. You were so great to get me my job and all. I love the apartment too. Even my ma thinks you should raise the rent—"

"Not now, Linnie. We'll talk about that another time."

"He won't raise the rent," Linnie said to Divinity. "He never does. I don't know how you make any money, Jake."

"Is that right?" Diverted, Divinity looked at him, certain that the ne'er-do-well of the county was embarrassed. "Tell us how many other recipients there are to your largesse."

Linnie pursed her lips. "I don't know, but Jake owns places here in the city and in some of the towns that he lets people have for almost nothing—"

"Linnie! Linnie . . ." He lowered his voice. "Let's talk about your friend Janis."

Divinity smiled. "Right. We'll talk about your real estate another time."

"Will we?" Jake was annoyed. Just because Divinity was beautiful and sexy didn't mean he'd open up to her about his . . . properties. Maybe after she married him.

"What are you grinning about, Jake?"

Her suspicious query deepened his amusement. "I'll tell you later."

Linnie looked from one to the other, puzzled. "I guess I don't know any more about this, Jake. But Janis had a journal she kept. She wanted to be a newspaper reporter one day." Linnie's chin lifted. "Janis took classes at William Smith and she had good marks. I didn't send the journal to her mother because she probably would have burned it. She didn't get along with Janis." Linnie chewed her lower lip. "I—I haven't been able to read it because . . . because . . ."

"It would hurt," Jake said.

"Yeah."

"Would you let me read it?" He gestured to Divinity. "Maybe it would be useful to Divinity, too."

Linnie stared at Jake, then eyed Divinity. She nodded. "I'd like to help Isaac. I can mail it to you, Jake."

"How would it be if I came by the apartment tonight and picked it up?"

"Fine." Linnie pushed back her chair. "I should get back to work. It was nice meeting you, Ms. Brown—"

"Divinity."

"Divinity." Linnie put out her hand, her smile shy. "I hope you win. I know the Meistersaengers. They put a porch on for my grandmother some years ago. They're nice people."

"It was good to meet you, Linnie. Thanks for your interest and your help."

Jake helped Linnie on with her coat, collecting her purse, gloves, and scarf for her. "I'll walk her down to the store and be right back."

Divinity nodded.

Jake buttoned his jacket, taking Linnie's order from Bernie. Outside the wind hit them like a frozen fist. Heads down they trudged the half a block to the store.

In the sheltered doorway, Jake waved to the people inside. "I'll pick up that journal tonight if it's all right, Linnie."

"That's fine, Jake." She reached up and kissed his

cheek. "Butch called my brother and said you're sweet on the lawyer. Are you?"

Jake was about to deny it. He opened his mouth, closed it, then said, "Yeah. Maybe I am."

Linnie laughed. She was about to enter the store, then she turned around and called to Jake before he could leave. "Come in a minute. I just remembered I brought the journal here along with some other things after we had a break-in. I was afraid I'd lose the last link I had to Janis. Not that burglars care about journals, but—"

"What break-in?" Jake asked as he closed the door behind him.

She winced. "You think I should've called you—"

"Damn straight."

"It wasn't a big deal, Jake. Some kid from Canandaigua broke into a few places on the block. Mine was one of them. He took my VCR—"

"I'll replace it."

"My insurance took care of it. Don't worry. My neighbor put new locks on for me."

"Send me the bill. I want to know more about this, Linnie."

"Jake." She shook her head. "You worry too much. Sam and his wife live down the street if I need someone. No big deal." She went behind the counter, reaching inside a drawer, and pulled out a faux-leather book.

"I don't like this, Linnie," Jake said as he took the journal from her. "You should have told me about the break-in."

"Jake—"

"Good for you, Jake," Sam Doyle, the owner of the store, said. "I told her to tell you when it happened. Tell Lithcomb to watch her place for a while. He's sweet on Linnie anyway." Sam grinned when Linnie turned fiery red and glared at him.

"I will." Jake kissed her cheek and waved good-bye. He shoved the book in his pocket and left, trotting head down against the cold, back to the café. "More coffee," he called to Bernie when he entered.

"Hey, Jake, you could frost your—"

"Yeah, yeah. How are you, Marty?" Jake asked the beefy man at the counter. "Sure is cold out there." He turned his back and went to sit with Divinity. "You can stop laughing now," he told her.

"Was I doing that?"

"You've been doing that since we met."

She nodded. "You're just a caution, Jake Blessing," she said, imitating the county twang. She sobered when she saw what he pulled from his jacket. "The journal?"

He nodded.

They finished their food and left, heading back to The Arbor. Though they talked about many things, their minds were on the journal.

They read it together, exchanging the numbered pages from the loose-leaf notebook. Outside of an occasional muttered curse, they said little.

"Quite a revelation," Divinity said when they'd finished.

Jake laced his hands behind his head. "I guess everybody knew there were nasty game players in the county, using guns as toys and booze for Dutch coverage. I didn't think they went as far as these sex games. Downright kidnapping and rape. Why didn't the girls come forward?"

"Fear is one of the best ways of immobilizing a crime victim."

He leaned forward, elbows on his knees. "I can't believe I didn't know about this." He shook his head. "Maybe I didn't want to know."

"Don't lash yourself, Jake. None of us think that people we know can be capable of viciousness, even when we read about it in the papers or hear it on the news."

"I caught Janis's fear when I read this." He tapped the journal. "Maybe she told Linnie she wasn't afraid, but I think she was."

Divinity nodded. "So do I. She was a sweet girl and too gullible."

"Those two other names in the journal itch at me too," Jake said. "Wendy Laidlaw and Darcy Lynch. According to Janis, they were strangers to the area."

"I saw that. I wonder if their names were run through the national list of Missing Persons. Even if no one knew them around here, there could be a connection elsewhere."

"It's a hole we didn't have. If we keep digging, we could find more. We'll work on it, Divinity." He stood and moved behind her, his hands massaging her shoulders. "You've been great. You're Isaac's best shot. He believes it, so does his family. So do I."

When he pressed his mouth against her hair, Divinity closed her eyes. She should move away from him, but it was too comforting to lean back against that warm body.

"You're on edge," he said.

She nodded, turning. "Actually I've always been like this when dealing with a case. Nerves I guess. I wish I had more information. The sketchy autopsy report I got from the crime lab wasn't as much help as I'd thought it would be. I—" A yawn interrupted her.

His arms went around her. When she stiffened, he exerted just enough pressure to bring her closer. "Comfort. That's all you need, Divinity. That's what I'm offering."

She exhaled, letting her body go lax against his, her eyes closing. How long they stood like that, she didn't know. All she felt was an increasing warmth, a loosening of the knots her nerves had tied themselves into, an unwinding of her body and mind.

Slowly she became aware of more. Only a child wouldn't have felt the hardening of his body. What stunned her was her response to it. She wanted to whisper that she needed him, that she didn't care that it would be a one-night stand. He was what she wanted. All her silent warnings that she'd be a fool to begin something that might be meaningless, that could distract her from the necessary focus she needed for Isaac's case, didn't move her. They didn't quiet the sultry desire pulsing through her.

"Got to go," she choked out, shoving out of his

grasp. She winged out the door, not looking back at him.

Jake faced the doorway, fighting for breath, his lower body hard and aching. Clenching and unclenching his fists, he spoke to the empty room. "One day we're going to talk, and more, Divinity Brown."

Later that night, after they'd shared a silent dinner, Jake knew Divinity was restlessly pacing her bedroom. He wouldn't have noticed anything with his blinds drawn, but he'd left them open and his corner window let him see a slash of one of her windows. Her light was on, and he could see her moving back and forth like a caged animal. He intended to ignore her, but the pacing went on too long. He left his bedroom and strode down the hall, rapping on her door.

She opened it, looking puzzled. "What?"

"You keep this up, you'll be a dishrag tomorrow. The hot tub for you, then bed. I'll bring you up something."

"Just tea."

"Go ahead."

She nodded. Before she could ask him if he intended to use the hot tub with her, he'd left. Her heart bumped her ribs at the thought of being in all that bubbling hot water with Jake. Erotic as hell.

Sighing, she put on her suit, then walked to the master suite where Jake was staying. Yawning, she went through his bedroom to the huge bathroom and the hot tub. Jake had already turned it on.

She climbed into the wood-framed tub and let herself sink into the churning water. Leaning her head back, she tried to keep her eyes open.


Jake had no intention of intruding. Divinity needed the relaxation that the hot tub would give her. By his watch it had been twenty minutes since she'd gone to his suite. She'd be ready for her tea by now, no doubt in her own room. His imagination could picture her rising from the tub, like Venus from the sea. He swallowed, closing his eyes and counting to ten, trying to force his aroused body to focus on anything else. When he tapped on her door, there was no answer. He put the tea down on a hall table and opened the door. She wasn't there.

Puzzled, he picked up the tray and turned back to his own suite. Crossing the bedroom, he thought he heard a sound. He peeked into the bathroom. She was still in the hot tub.

Pausing near the tub, he studied her. She was half-asleep, flushed and relaxed, and the sight of her had his heart hammering in his chest. Placing the tea tray on the raised platform that based the hot tub, he leaned over and put his mouth close to her ear.

"Tea is served, and it's time to get out of there."

Her eyes flew open. Her body slid sideways, the sudden movement causing a wave that splashed into her mouth. "Wha . . . ?"

"You've been in there long enough." He reached for a bath sheet as she stood up. Her racing suit delineated her body, long, slender, and beautiful, and he wanted her. When her mouth curved into the most sensuous smile he'd ever seen, he couldn't get enough air.

"Thanks for the towel," she said over her shoulder as he draped it around her.

He inhaled her warm sweetness, swallowed hard, and picked up the tray. "You can drink this in the bedroom if you like."

Swathed in the towel, she preceded him.

"Over here," he said, putting the tea tray down on the desk. He glared at the slight tremor in his hands.

"Something wrong?" she asked at his back.

"Plenty." His smile twisted when he looked at her over his shoulder. "That you're beautiful and I want you might be the underlying problem."

"Oh."

He wheeled to face her. "Don't feel threatened by my big mouth. You have nothing to fear from me."

"I'm not afraid."

"Good."

They faced each other, silently crossing bridge after bridge, letting them go down in flames.

She put out her hand. His met it halfway and they linked.

"This might not be a good idea, Jake."

"It's the best I have to offer right now."

"I see."

"Do you?"

Both voices were husky, hesitant.

"I—I haven't been . . ." she stammered. "That is, I don't think I want to get involved. I'm not sure . . ."

"You never said a truer word, or words," he murmured. "I'll go if that's what you want. I'd rather stay."

"I'd like you to stay." She swallowed. "After all, it's your room."

"Right."

She glanced at the desk. "Tea's getting cold."

"I'll make more." When he caught her to him, she wound her arms around his neck.

"This could be an outstanding blunder," she whispered.

"I don't give a damn," he muttered against her cheek. "You're lovely."

All the reasons she had for holding back from him were still valid. She'd come to The Arbor for privacy, for R and R. The last thing she needed was a relationship, especially one that was virtually guaranteed to be brief. Taking on a new case was bad enough. Jake was a complication that could screw that up as well as her life. All that was true, but the arguments didn't seem to have the same punch anymore. She touched his chin. "You've told me that . . . that I'm lovely, you know."

"I intend to keep doing it." He cupped her jaw, kissing the corner of her mouth. "I want you."

She took a deep breath. Her better sense told her to lie. "I feel the same," she said instead.

"I hear the 'but' in your voice."

Her smile tilted. "I want you, Jake." She inhaled the sweetness when he whispered the same in her ear.

"There's Isaac, though. I owe him full concentration. You and I know there's a long way to go."

He nodded, regret limning his smile. He lifted her hand, kissing the palm, then each finger. "Fair enough. Promise me . . ."

She saw the arrested look on his face, how his eyes fixed on her fingers, narrowing in concentration. "What?"

"Actually, I was thinking about your fingernails. If you really got angry and felt threatened, you'd scratch and dig. Most women would. Didn't you say something about DNA testing on the autopsy report?"

Divinity nodded, alert.

"From what I've heard about Penny," he went on, "she was a pretty spirited young lady. She wouldn't back down with a payoff when she discovered she was pregnant. And if she were attacked, she'd fight back, if she had a chance. So there might be something under her fingernails. Wouldn't pathology have found that?"

Divinity nodded. "I didn't see anything about scrapings from under the victim's nails, but I only skimmed the autopsy report. I might've missed that." She turned to leave, her arousal forgotten in her eagerness to retrieve the autopsy report from the library. The bath sheet tripped her, and Jake caught her. She hauled in a breath.

"Thought you'd fall," he murmured against her ear.

"Thank you." When he kissed her cheek, she felt a roar somewhere in the vicinity of her ear. It was like being under Niagara Falls.

"This has nothing to do with the case," Jake said.

"Too bad," she whispered into his throat, as the towel slipped. "I think you're onto something with the DNA."

"We can check it tomorrow."

"We can get up early."

"That was my thought."

"Good one, Blessing."

"You're beautiful."

"So are you," she said dreamily, smiling when he chuckled.

"I thought I was more in control." He leaned back. "But I'm shaken."

"Something in the air," she suggested, loosening the buttons on his shirt.

He nodded, trying to get out of his clothes and hold on to her at the same time. "This isn't easy."

"Nothing good ever is." She kissed him, her mouth slanting over his, her hands cupping his face. "For a ne'er-do-well, you're a pretty thing."

He shook his head, his grin answering hers. "Cute, Divinity."

"Yeah. I'm a darling." Under her banter was a lacing of fear. If she let him get too close and then lost him, it would hurt more than anything in her past.

"You are darling," he said, "and I'm grateful you came to Yokapa County." He swept her up into his arms. "My bed okay?"

"Sure." She pressed her face close to his. "You must be damned strong. I'm no lightweight."

The phone rang. Jake muttered an epithet. Divinity

bit back a moan. It rang until the answering machine beside Jake's bed kicked in. "Jake, it's Darnell, on the site. Some creeps tried to break in. We didn't catch them, but we scared them off. I called the sheriff and—"

Jake picked up the phone as he let Divinity's feet slide to the floor. "Yeah. I'm here." He looked at Divinity, anger and frustration in his expression.

She felt the same frustration, though she couldn't help thinking of the old saw, "saved by the bell." Jake had aroused her more easily than anyone ever had. She'd wanted him more than she'd ever wanted anyone or anything. Jake Blessing had the power to hurt her. Instinct told her he could put her in a tailspin for a lifetime. Just maybe he was more than she could handle.

She wrapped the towel around herself again, waved to him, and left the room, feeling his eyes on her back.

# FIVE

"A rather dingy place, even for a pathology lab," Divinity said.

It was the morning after they had almost made love. Divinity had studied Penny Elgin-Brown's autopsy report again that morning, and had seen that the ME had sent various tissues he'd collected before the body was stolen to a man named LeRoy Wilkins. When she had asked Jake, he'd said he knew LeRoy, who was a renowned pathologist, quite well. He had intended to suggest that they talk to him that day. Jake had called LeRoy, at his home, explaining why Divinity wanted to see him. LeRoy had told them he'd meet them at his lab.

"It might seem dingy," Jake said in response to her comment, "but wait until you meet LeRoy. He doesn't need sunshine. He makes his own. Not many know his worth because he keeps to himself, but he's so damned brilliant Cornell Medical School didn't know how to handle him. He mastered most of the great skills of medicine, including reconstructive surgery and neurosurgery, to name a few. He's a genius . . . who prefers forensic pathology to a fancy office on Park Avenue."

"Another of your friends." It wasn't a question.

Jake nodded. "Most people forget he's down here. When they built the other county complex, they all but misplaced him. Then they told him he could move into the new buildings, but they'd cut his equipment room to the bone. He made them list the expenditures, then he told them he'd take the money, stay in the old building, and add a few amenities of his own. Most of the police cases coming his way are from Albany or D.C. To a select group of law enforcement, he's a godsend. To most people he's the invisible man."

"Did you do his renovating?"

His head swung her way. "How did you know?"

"A wild guess."

He was still studying her when he pushed open half of the double doors, which were wide enough to accommodate any size of machine or gurney. "LeRoy?" he called.

"Yep. Back here. That you, Jake?"

"How'd you know?"

"You're the only one who visits me." The low laughter had no self-pity.

"No one knows your worth then," Jake said.

Only Divinity caught his words. For a moment she was angered with Jake Blessing. He was filling too many holes in her life too fast. What if she lost him?

He was getting too close, revealing virtues she held dear—principle, compassion, dedication. All that stupid stuff no one discusses for fear of being thought weird. Jake never mentioned any of it. He probably didn't even know they were woven into his innermost fabric, yet he possessed high ethics couched in the sexiest body she'd ever seen. She had to find *something* wrong with him.

"Are you doing something gross," Jake asked, "or can I bring my friend around to your table?" He spoke toward towering bookcases that extended out from the wall, and were crammed with pamphlets, books, and papers from top to bottom.

"Come ahead," LeRoy answered. "I've told you many times you're too squeamish to see the beauty of blood and tissue, Jake. If you took the time to study those things, you'd feel differently."

"No, I wouldn't."

"Sure you would. I guarantee it."

Jake rolled his eyes as Divinity stifled a laugh. Taking her hand, he led her around the Berlin Wall of paper and chuckled when her mouth dropped. It was even worse on the other side. In the middle of the chaos was a desk. Behind it stood a gurney with a body on it, swathed in a sheet. A cherubic, rotund person looked up at her through thick glasses, his smile showing dimples in his elfin face. "Hi. You must be Isaac's lawyer. I understand Jake's bonkers about you."

"Hey!"

Divinity laughed, then bit it back when Jake glared at her.

"Well? You said you found something?" Jake's truculent tone made LeRoy's grin widen.

The cherub got off his high stool and went to the desk, pawing through hillocks of papers. "I got lucky, Jake. I got a body"—he jerked his head toward the gurney—"of a girl who was supposed to be a hit-and-run victim. Her name was Wendy Laidlaw. I got her because all they were going to do was bury her." LeRoy looked at Jake. "I've kept her here, preserved, because too much about her doesn't fit the pattern of a hit-and-run. When you described Ms. Brown's suspicions, I talked to the ME. He was glad to give me all the tests they had on the Elgin-Brown girl. I've found some similarities. I thought I might."

"What do you mean?" Divinity asked.

"This poor young woman wasn't killed by a car. She was strangled, then run over."

"Are you sure?" Divinity could hardly breathe. "What are the similarities?"

"I've read the autopsy report on the Elgin-Brown woman." He shook his head. "It's not much, just some initial conclusions the ME made before the body was stolen. There was a comment about the victim's neck I thought was interesting. The ME described the same abrasions I found on the Laidlaw woman. Too bad there wasn't time for more testing." His visage turned grim. "If I hadn't decided to do what needed to be done in the new lab, if I'd brought the Elgin-Brown woman and her baby here, the cadavers might never have been stolen. But, I got what I needed." His grin made him look like the Cheshire cat.

Jake looked at Divinity. "LeRoy's a detail man. He keeps records on everything that has to do with pathology, wounds, ailments, blood types. Great hobby."

LeRoy chuckled. He walked over to the gurney, then looked back at them. "This is the Laidlaw girl. You're not going to faint, are you?"

Divinity shook her head. "It's not my first time in a crime lab."

"I might," Jake muttered. "Go ahead."

Outside of a few deep breaths and some foot shifting, the visitors did nothing while LeRoy studied the cadaver, then he waved them to his side.

"Right here." LeRoy pointed. "See? Looks as though her fingernails were cleaned. Same thing on the Elgin-Brown woman, according to the autopsy report. They found some scrapings, though. I took the few they had. Luckily for me they hadn't done anything with them, so I was able to run tests on them anyway. I've done the same with the Laidlaw woman."

"The same cleaning was done on both women," Divinity said. She leaned over the cadaver.

"Yep. Poor things."

"But the cleaning wasn't thorough? You have scrapings from both?"

"I do." He indicated a notebook and large box.

"Can this help us?" Divinity crossed her fingers.

He turned back to the desk and shuffled the papers. "I found enough similarity to convince me that what was under the nails of this one was more than a close match to what was taken from Penny Elgin-Brown. I got the sample of the accused's blood too. It's not the same. DNA can be similar in some people, and I'd testify it was close. But I'd stake my reputation it's not the same." His lips pursed. "It's more than a hunch, Ms. Brown."

"And you would testify to that?"

"Sure. I know I'm right." His cherubic smile went over her and Jake. "And I'm considered one of the top experts in the country on DNA."

"The best," Jake said.

Divinity exhaled. "Reasonable doubt. That's all I need." She looked up at Jake. "I think this is it." She turned back to LeRoy. "If I presented the theory that the fingernails could've been cleaned by someone to hide the real culprit, could you back me up?"

He shook his head. "Not with facts, but I could tell the judge how I felt about what I had to work with . . . and that I could've done more if the bodies and samples had been brought to me directly, instead of to the ME's office. It wouldn't have been stolen from here." He jerked his head at Wendy Laidlaw's body. "At least I got her. I've finished with her now."

"I'll take care of her," Jake said.

Divinity winced. He was doing it again. Getting under her guard with his kindness. She could just hit him. If he was that good, such a heart's-desire, a perfect man, how come no one had snapped him up yet? Was he too good to be true? Dammit, she might snag him herself if he didn't watch his step.

"What's wrong?" Jake asked her as LeRoy began filling out forms so that the body could be released to the Nellis Funeral Home and Mortuary. The bills would be sent to Jacob Blessing.

Divinity considered not answering, then thought, to hell with it. Let him hear it. "Are you deliberately trying to undermine me so I'll invite you into my bed?"

Flummoxed, Jake stared at her, his mouth falling open. "Ah . . . that . . . ah . . . Why—why not?"

"Ah-ha. I thought so." She poked her index finger in his chest. "Don't push me too far, Blessing. You might find yourself in a bind. See how you'd like it if you woke up married!" She nodded curtly, then stalked around him to the desk where LeRoy was writing.

"I'll be damned," Jake muttered. "I must've done something right. Wonder what it was."

Late the next morning Divinity explored the Blessing estate, needing a break from her work on Isaac's case. She thought she found a small cemetery, but the snow was so deep, she couldn't be sure. None of the headstones showed through the drifts.

Clumping through the thick snow, she went around to the front of the house. Seeing the crèche, she considered taking it down. The activity might obliterate the thoughts of Jake that tumbled through her mind. Two nights before they'd almost made love, and she'd wanted him with an ache that was still with her.

She looked up at the sky as though the expanse held the answers to all her questions. Jake? Isaac? Her future?

"Don't think about it," she muttered to herself.

*Sure*, an inner voice answered. *Easy for you to say*.

She circled the crèche, trying to figure what was the best way to begin.

"You might need these," Jake said from behind her.

"Oh?" She turned. As always she was struck by how handsome and sexy he was.

"Tools."

She couldn't hold back a smile, barely looking at the sled that held a bulging canvas bag. "Good idea."

"At least the wind has let up." Without warning he stooped, scooped up some snow, and threw it underhand at her.

"Wanna play?" She bent down and grabbed a handful. "Ah, good packing." She rounded out her snowball and pitched it at Jake. He ducked, and it missed him. His struck her on the arm, eliciting a howl of outrage. Laughing, he took off toward the back of the house. She stalked him. When he disappeared, she hunted, following his footsteps, rounding to the front of the house again.

"Hey! I'm here." He rose from behind the crèche and fired a snowball. Divinity ducked and shot back. She yelped with joy when she connected.

"I give up. Surrender." He came from behind the crèche, walking over to her. He circled her with one arm and brought up the snow he had in the other hand. "Fooled you."

She closed her eyes and flinched. Then she nearly fainted. Instead of the face washing she was expecting, she got the hottest, sweetest kiss of her life. His mouth opened on hers, tasting and testing her lips and tongue.

Too wanting not to give back, her mouth parted. The invasion of his tongue left her knees weak, her body slack against his. The winter cold had no effect on the fierce heat they generated.

Swaying in the emotional hurricane that carried them far beyond any snow, lake, or sky, they possessed each other. Cocooned in the newness of passion, emotion, compassion, tenderness, Divinity could have stayed in his arms forever.

He moved back first, about half an inch. "Your kisses are as potent as moonshine, Divinity."

She gulped air, trying not to see three of him, while her heart trip-hammered in her chest. "Don't expect to melt me with those flowery words, Jake."

"I'll think of more."

"I think we should take down the crèche."

"Right."

Neither moved.

Leaning back a bit, she studied him. "This could be all wrong."

"Doesn't feel that way to me."

She shook her head, figuring she'd done all she could to fight him off. "It's too cold to just stand here." He grinned and she shivered, but not with cold.

His eyes seemed to peel the winter clothing from her body. Not able to hold that hot gaze, she looked around her. "This is a beautiful place."

"Yes, it is, but I'd rather talk about you," he said,

his voice gentle, his hand cupping her cheek. "I'm not going to rush you, Divinity."

"We're past the rushing part."

"Right." He lowered his face to hers again. "I don't want you to have regrets."

"I won't." She patted his cheek. "My time with you has been special. I wouldn't regret it in ten lifetimes."

"Neither would I." He kissed her again. "Though you might be sorry you admitted it."

"Oh? Why?"

"Because I'm starting, as of now, to push for something longer. We're talking years."

She blinked and swallowed. "Fine. That'll take some discussion. In the meantime we can take the crèche down and put it away."

His burst of laughter made her smile.

"Let's do it," he said. He opened the bag of tools, then knelt in front of the crèche, studying it. "I'd better do this right. Harlan will give me hell if I don't."

"You're one tough landlord."

He grinned. "I don't push my luck."

"You're a great guy, Jake Blessing," she said. "Let me work on this side." At his nod, she took a wrench and hammer from the canvas bag.

It was a slow beginning. Gradually, and with care, they loosened the outer frozen bolts with wrenches.

"Shouldn't we put these in something?" Divinity asked as she took one piece apart.

Jake nodded toward the sled. "Put them on that. There are wooden cases in the barn where we store the sections."

She went back to work, her insides bubbling like hot ginger ale. It was madness. She felt more girlish than when she'd been a teenager. In her whole life she'd never felt so strong, or so feminine.

Jake watched her for a minute, enjoying the sight. She belonged there, in the snows in front of The Arbor, overlooking Cayuga Lake. It seemed like old knowledge he'd dredged up from a filing cabinet in his brain. She was part of the scenery he pictured in his future. It could take a great deal of convincing to get her to stay, but she was well worth the time. His smile widened. At her feet was a crowbar, much too heavy a tool for the teakwood crèche. She glanced into the tool bag and began removing assorted screwdrivers and wrenches. These were placed in a neat row on a wrought-iron bench nearby. He couldn't stop watching her. She looked beautiful, her face glowing in the frosty air.

As though she'd felt his scrutiny, she looked up, her smile as rosy as her cheeks. "Get to work."

"Get a whip."

She lifted her chin. "I might."

"Sounds exciting." When she blushed, he chuckled.

She whirled around. Grabbing a section of the crib, she tugged, grunting. "This should give way easily. The other side did." She ground her teeth, her face reddening as she pulled harder.

"Wait. Let me." Jake went around behind her, his arms cupping hers, her hair brushing his chin. When she leaned back to give him a better view, the touch of her body burned him. His blood steamed. "You're beautiful, Divinity." She didn't stiffen or pull away, but he sensed a restraint. "It's not a come-on, just the truth." He exhaled heavily. "Of course I admit I'd like to come on to you. Can't help it." When she eyed him over her shoulder, he kissed her nose. "How about a deal?"

"What kind?"

The huskiness in her voice had his body hardening. "Very simple. I want you. You know that. We would've made love two nights ago if we hadn't been interrupted. You know that too." He hesitated.

"Go on."

"If you don't want a lifetime commitment, we can go week by week. What do you say?"

"I say you can move pretty fast."

Her sweet grin, the coy tilt of her head had him gulping air. "You're powerful, attorney lady."

"Are you working on the crèche?"

"I am. See." He twisted the joining just a hair and it came free. "These have been dovetailed with the old-fashioned tenons. See? They can be pulled and turned. No nails."

"Wonderful."

"You're blushing."

"Cold weather does that."

"What were you thinking?"

"About—about joinings."

He groaned. "So was I."

She turned and pressed her face into the scarf around his neck, chuckling. The wind was picking up again, probably dropping the chill to subzero.

For some time neither moved, the silence laced with air rattling through frosted trees.

"What are you thinking about now?" Jake whispered, rising to his feet and bringing her with him. "Tongue and groove?"

When she glanced at him, her eyes were alight, her mouth prim. "Along those lines. Incidentally, I have a few questions."

"Fire away."

"Can you provide references?"

He sucked in a breath of laughter. "Maybe. Yeah, I guess I can get up a list of people who'd give me positive marks."

"Dorothy Lally?"

"She might qualify her statements." He leaned back. "I'm willing to go the extra step. I've had all my shots, and I'm disease free, except for an occasional sneeze and cough." He tapped her nose. "You don't have to give me any proof. I'll take your word you're the same."

"Hmm. And you're supposed to be a good businessman?"

"I am." He touched her skin with his lips, just a dusting. His heart started to pound. "Are you the committing kind?"

"No. Not anymore." She hauled in a deep breath. "How about you?"

"I can commit, I guess. Never have, but I'd give it a go." He paused. "But we've kind of committed already, Divinity. Verbal agreements count. When we take it to the next step, it will be something very special."

"What if you want space, Jake?"

"Not to worry. I won't."

She didn't want to fight him, but a well-developed wariness had her continuing. "I might need some."

"Take all the space you need."

"Thanks," she said dryly. "You know, I am terribly busy with the case . . ."

"If the case were out of the way, how would you feel?"

The pause stretched, then snapped like a rubber band.

"It—it could be interesting." She wet her lips. "If we start slow. I could do that."

"We're already pretty sure sex could be great between us," he said, angling his body so his back caught the icy wind.

"We do know that."

"That's a step in the right direction. We have the same commitment to Isaac."

"There's that. I guess you could say we have a leg up." She buried her laughter in his jacket.

"Nice, making fun of what we have."

"You're laughing, too, Jake."

"I am. Actually I've been smiling since we met."

She leaned back and looked up at him. "Not when you were eating my chicken salad sandwich."

"My mouth was too full to stretch that way." He kissed her. "We'd be sensational. Give it a try."

Her smile faded, her chest bursting with a brand-new emotion, a blossoming feeling she'd never known existed. "I guess I could handle being part of a two-some."

"I could, too, Divinity Brown." He tightened his hold, putting his mouth over hers. He hadn't released his grip on the teakwood joining. As the kiss increased, so did the pressure on the wood. With a creaky sound, something snapped.

Divinity pulled back, her eyes dark, her mouth parted. "You broke it."

"What?"

"The crèche. I heard it snap."

Jake blinked. "Who gives a damn?" he muttered.

"You do. It's precious."

"Right." He looked over her shoulder, keeping her locked to his side with one arm. She saw him scowl.

"What?"

"I guess I did break it. This is the first time I've tried to put it away. Harlan usually—"

"Wait." She turned in his arms.

"What?"

They both bent over the joining. "It's like a little drawer, Jake. There's paper in there."

"Yeah. I see it. What is it?" He stopped her when she would have removed her gloves. "Uh-uh. Not here. Too cold to keep your gloves off for long. Don't worry about it. I'll bring some of the boys over this afternoon. They'll take care of everything and put the crèche away properly. Let's get out of here. The wind's sharpening again. The kitchen will be warm. Maybe Harlan's baked something."

"Maybe he won't give you any." She laughed when

he groaned. Stuffing the small paper in her glove, she was glad Jake kept his arm around her as the wind crackled through the leafless trees.

Inside Jake helped her off with her coat, then he put his arms around her. "I'm a good prospect. I thought you should know that. I have a job, a house, a truck, and a business that's not deeply in debt."

"Wonderful. How about your teeth, eyes, and hair? Do they need any work?"

He grinned. "You mean we'll have a dental plan?"

"Spunky little devil, aren't you?"

"Yes, ma'am." He leaned down, setting his mouth over hers. The kiss was lazy, sweet, and hot enough to bring the lake to a boil. "Think about it."

"I will." Divinity coughed to clear the squeak from her voice.

In the kitchen Jake went for the coffee, picking up a still-warm croissant as he passed.

"No crumbs on the floor," Harlan said. "You help yourself, Miss Divinity. Today's my day to volunteer at the House of Concern. I'll be back to make supper."

"Be careful. There could be slippery patches on the highway," Jake said.

"I taught you how to drive, Junior. Remember?"

Jake nodded.

Divinity listened to the exchange, thinking the relationship between the two men was more like father and son, than employer and employee. She settled herself at the breakfast bar with a cup of fragrant coffee, then opened up the paper she'd found in the crèche. "I guess it's old from the rusty look of the ink, and the paper is pretty fragile." She studied the writing, which had curlicues on the letters, common in past times. "Hmm. I'm not sure about this, but there seems to be a reference to a man buried in the family plot—"

"That's on the ridge behind the house." Jake ambled over with a plate of croissants.

Divinity was delighted. "I think I might have been near it. Do you know exactly where the cemetery is even in the snow?"

His grin was lopsided. "Sure. My mother picked out my plot."

The vinegary humor wasn't lost on her. "The cemetery's still being used then?"

"Not recently. My father chose to have his ashes spread on the lake."

He sat on the stool next to her, and they stumbled through the blurry, smeared writing on the paper. "Amazing," Jake said. "The name is Brown, I'm sure of that. Maybe that's our ghost."

She nodded. "It's bizarre enough that I'm a Brown, and the murder victim in Isaac's case was one. Now, maybe the Blessing cemetery has one more." She handed the paper to him. "Would you like to keep it? If someone can decipher more of this, it might connect to your family."

"You keep it. It might connect to the case in some weird way." His smile was strained. "I know enough about my family."

She hesitated, not wanting to pry, but needing to know more about the man who'd become such a large part of her life in such a short time. Her mind hunted for the right words.

"What?" He leaned toward her. "Ask me anything, Divinity."

"I wondered about your parents," she blurted out.

"Ahh, there's a subject. It's not the easiest one."

"Then forget—"

"But I want to tell you."

"Oh."

Jake allowed his thoughts to go back. "I was not 'der wunderkind,' as anyone in Yokapa County would tell you." His gaze slipped away from her to the wall. "I loved The Arbor as a child. I romped all over the grounds and through the house. I guess it started to change when I was ready for kindergarten, or maybe that's when I first noticed my mother's antipathy toward her role as wife and mother. Nothing seemed to please her. Actually most things my father and I did enraged her. Lucky for me we had a housekeeper, Harlan's aunt, Mrs. Weeks, who could control my mother's tantrums to some degree. She was able to keep me out of my mother's way most of the time."

"Was your mother ill?" Divinity's heart shrank at the thought of the lonely child who didn't know why his mother disliked him.

"Maybe. No one ever said that, if they knew. My father never discussed her after she left us."

"How old were you?"

"Fourteen. I was fifteen when I overheard Naomie Weeks talking on the phone to a friend about my mother running away with Roger Callan." Jake's mouth twisted. "He'd been my mother's lover for years, they said."

"That's rough."

"I guess." He looked in her eyes. "The truth is I was glad when she was gone. It was quiet."

"So you felt guilty when you found out about her death."

He touched her cheek. "That's about it." He straightened on the stool. "I was considered recalcitrant. I was taken out of public school and enrolled in Crossfield Academy. That was supposed to straighten me out. Maybe it did. I learned a good bit about Shakespeare, guns, and handling myself."

"So much for the formative years." Divinity touched his hand, and he turned it over and grasped hers. She could feel his loneliness as though it were an ice blanket he'd handed her. "You played football, I'll bet."

"Lacrosse and basketball. Sports kept me out of trouble, most of the time."

"When you weren't getting shot at by Sandy Garret."

"Right." He pulled her hand to his mouth, kissing the palm. "It disappointed my father when I went to Hobart instead of Cornell, his alma mater."

"And you didn't choose law."

He nodded. "When I left Hobart, I hitchhiked around Europe, came home and did the same thing here. I got into construction work in California to pay the rent. I liked it, bought a small company there, and was staying even. When my father became ill, I sold out and came east. I started a business here, and believe me when I tell you it took time to get it off the ground. It came out of the red a few months before my father died." He looked away again. "I couldn't tell him that. He was too sick."

There was a wealth of wishing in his voice. Divinity knew without asking that it had hurt not to be able to show his father he could make it on his own. "It would have been painful to stay here after your father died."

"Yeah."

"This is a beautiful place, Jake. The Medina stone, the lovely turrets, the terraces. No matter how gloomy it gets outside, that terra-cotta-colored stone glows."

He smiled.

"And where could you find glazed and leaded windows of such quality and shape? Chancel, triangular, coved, round, long . . ." She shook her head, noting his crooked smile. "What?"

"You've got a good heart, Divinity. Trying to distract me from my not-so-comforting memories is very sweet of you."

"A lawyer? Sweet? Did you ever hear the one about the difference between a skunk and a lawyer dead on the road?"

"No."

"There are skid marks in front of the skunk."

He smiled. "That's not you, though. And I'd rather talk about you, than me."

"I want to hear more about your childhood, unless it hurts too much."

"It doesn't, not anymore. My father was a stern man, and not given to gestures of affection, but I knew he cared for me. And I loved him. He was honorable." Jake grinned. "And a lifelong conservative. We always had arguments about my liberalism, but they were friendly and I learned a great deal about jurisprudence from him." His grin touched her. "I still prefer construction."

"Good choice. I probably should've made the same one."

"Uh-uh. You're a born advocate, lady. If my father were here, he'd say the same." Jake looked up at the ceiling. "Those last days we spent a great deal of time together, talking. I regret now I didn't talk to him about my mother. I was afraid it would hurt him."

Divinity nodded.

"After he died I used a portion of the estate to buy up properties, renovating some and renting or selling."

"Like Linnie's place."

"Yeah. I started building condos, too, here and in Florida. It's paying off."

"Harlan says you've done work for Habitat for Humanity."

"Some."

"He says a lot."

"Harlan exaggerates."

"No, he doesn't."

Jake picked up his coffee. "Enough about me. I

think before we got sidetracked I was telling you about the cemetery."

"And I'd love to research this." She pointed to the paper they'd taken from the crèche. "I'm too tied up with Isaac's case to get involved now. Maybe once the case gets settled I'll look into it."

Jake shrugged. "Sure. As I recall there are two sections in the cemetery. One is pretty old and it might not be our family. Could be the original landowners used it."

"It's silly to get so caught up in this when Isaac's trial is uppermost in my mind, but—"

"The ghost probably told you to go for it. Right?" He grimaced when she seemed to pull back from him. "Sorry. I forget you've got as many prickly edges as I have."

"You don't have any," she muttered.

He nodded. "Yes, I do. I've just been at the game of 'pretend it doesn't matter' longer than you."

"I'm not sure I know what you mean."

"You know, the business of being the outsider, the ne'er-do-well of the county."

She inclined her head. "You don't seem hurt by it when Harlan calls you that."

"I'm not. He'd step in front of a bus for me . . . he and Dorothy and Pepper Lally. There're other people who jab and cut for sport. I don't like it. It could get to me, if I let it. Learning to keep a blank look on my face took practice." He moved closer, kissing her forehead. "Never let them see you bleed."

"And some of the remarks aren't meant to hurt."

"Yeah. Like now."

"Fair enough. As to your remark about the ghost . . ." She shook her head. "I don't know how to explain it, but I'm sure she was sending me a message. I just don't know what it would be." She bit her lip. "And maybe the name Surratt means nothing. The page could just have turned from a draft, the door opening or something like that."

Jake leaned back, watching her. "You don't believe that."

"No, I don't."

"Well, think about it. What would be important to you? If she's really trying to communicate, it might be because of the name Brown, or that Surratt was connected with the death of Lincoln, or just because you're dealing with the Civil War."

"I wish the ghost were telling me more about Isaac's case than the Civil War."

"Maybe she's trying to tell you about the Civil War and today."

Divinity straightened, a lacing of excitement on her face. "Like linking something, tying it together, making a connection from past to present. I hadn't thought of that." She smiled at him. "At least it's better than no theory. What do we know about Mrs. Surratt. She kept a house where conspirators met and she was hanged. Why Surratt? Why me? What does the ghost want me to know?"

He shook his head. "I think we should keep an

open mind. No one's an expert on ghosts, except the spirits themselves."

Divinity patted his cheek, her eyes alight. "You know what's nice about you. You're not a cynic."

"Stop saying sweet things."

"Why?"

"Because you could be responsible for my long hospital stay."

"You're not sick."

He kissed her, keeping it light. "You should have noticed by now I'm having a heart attack," he said against her mouth.

"Only fair," she murmured. "So am I." He was a wonderful man. Tall. Handsome. Gentle. Was he for real? Nothing in her life had prepared her for Jake. Instinct told her that if she pulled back from him, she would lose all the true feelings she'd longed for and sought all her life.

"Divinity," he said.

"Work," she whispered, her voice shaking.

Jake pulled back an inch. "Pragmatist."

She nodded. "I need to go over the notes I made at the pathology lab."

"If you present what LeRoy's given you in the hearing, you might not go to trial."

"I hope it works that way. I think there's enough similarities in what happened to the two women to point to Isaac's innocence, to convince the judge to throw out the case. If LeRoy testifies that Wendy Laidlaw died from strangulation, like Penny, we might have a chance. And Wendy Laidlaw was found on the thruway, not a road open to the Amish. How would Isaac have gotten her there? Certainly not in a wagon. It's not allowed."

Jake hugged her. "It makes sense. Divinity, you're wonderful."

"Thank LeRoy Wilkins."

"I will." He kissed her hard, then not so hard, then softer.

"But I need more in case it goes to trial. Garret is determined to bury Isaac, he's made that clear." She eyed Jake. "Would it make him a big man in the community?"

"I'm sure there are some who resent the Amish. They're very successful farmers. I'd say most people like and respect them, though. It wouldn't be a feather in Garret's cap to nail him. On the flip side, a win is a win, and I think he has political ambitions." Jake shook his head. "I don't think it's personal as much as it is political with Sandy, maybe giving him the boost he needs to run for governor."

"Great combination. Ambitious and smart."

"You've met him head-to-head, with confidence and aplomb so far. Keep at it."

"From what you've told me Mr. Garret is a more than worthy adversary, and he doesn't like to lose."

"It's true. That doesn't mean you won't beat him."

She nodded. "I think I can. I'd just be more comfortable with more material." She hesitated. "You believe I can win Isaac's case?"

Jake nodded. "I do." He slid off his stool and urged her to her feet. He clasped her hands; their bodies touched. He smiled down at her. "I don't consider the ghost as much of a miracle as you are."

She smiled. "I'm hardly in the same class as a manifestation."

He brought one of her hands to his mouth and kissed it. "No? Harlan went crazy with most of the lessors. You arrived, and he was ecstatic—"

"Ecstatic? I don't think so."

"Trust me, he was. Isaac had his back to the wall until you came along, a crackerjack lawyer. Happenstance? I don't think so." She was about to interject again, but he shook his head. "Linnie had some information that I'm damned sure she wouldn't have shared with any of our local shysters."

"I'm sure they'd be thrilled at your choice of words."

Jake shrugged. "I was beginning to think I knew women. Then you showed up, and I realized I didn't know beans."

"A veritable babe in the woods. That's Jake Blessing."

"Are you blushing because you don't believe me . . . or because you know it's true? It's a compliment, and the bare facts, ma'am." His smile twisted. "You're everything I could ever want. I think I knew it the first day, but I wasn't about to tell you then."

"Oh." She licked her lips. He shouldn't have told her now. She didn't have the stamina to be a trial lawyer and handle Jake Blessing at the same time. He'd just dropped the World Trade Center on her head, and he was being offhand about it.

"I'm baring my soul," he went on, "because I can't risk playing games with you. You could run anyway, or tell me to get lost, and I might never see you again." He looked pensive for a moment. "That's not true. I'd follow you anywhere." He inhaled. "Back to the subject of our relationship—"

"We have one?"

"I'm working on it. Let me get this said, please."

"Sorry."

"Okay. Now, I ran most of the variables on our relationship—"

"That word again."

"Divinity!"

"Sorry."

"Okay. I thought I might have a better chance with all my cards on the table."

He lifted her hand to his mouth again. "You aren't expected to sell the farm over this, or even be my free legal eagle forever. Just think about us in tandem, as a team—"

"Like the Belgian horses the Amish use?"

"Something like that. Just consider it, mull it over, then contact me, lady."

Shaky laughter spilled out of her. "You sound like Justifiable Jake, the used-car salesman."

He grinned. "Whatever it takes, I can be, attorney lady."

"Fair enough." She brought her other hand up over his. "I'm not sure I could handle anything, short- or long-term."

He looked down at their clasped hands. "Want to

give it a try? No locks on anything. Both of us have
outs . . . but I think we should be clear on how we
feel . . . if we do, or don't." He looked up at her.
"When we make love, it'll be the greatest moment of
my life. The most beautiful experience ever."

Honesty galloped past prudence. Divinity nodded.
"For me too."

"So we can take a crack at this?"

"I—I feel very attracted to you. No doubt of that.
Is it enough?"

"For now I'll take it." He stared into her eyes, then
moved back, freeing his hands, and sticking out the
right one. "You want to shake on the deal, Divinity
Brown?"

She put out her hand, then pulled it back. "Do I
get a six-month warranty?"

"I think I can manage that."

"CD player included?"

"You drive a hard bargain. Okay."

"Done." She took his hand and shook it.

Jake pulled her close again. "I wish we could start
now."

"Too much work. You know that."

"It won't always be that way," he said into her hair,
his eyes closed.

"No. We won't let it."

"I feel I've known you all my life."

She grinned. "Maybe you have."

"I know you better than people I've known all my
life."

She leaned back in his arms, nodding. "Strange, but

true." She reached up and touched his face, sighing. "I have to work."

"I know." He lifted her hand, his tongue scoring her palm.

Divinity was surprised when her legs carried her from the kitchen.

# SIX

Late that afternoon Divinity drove to the county jail to see Isaac. If the judge hadn't set bail so high, the Meistersaengers might've managed it. The family refused to use a bondsman, so Isaac had remained incarcerated.

As always, Divinity was astounded at the snowbanks on either side of the road. Neither the fields nor the lake could be seen. It was like driving in a tunnel.

When she returned, she hurried from the barn to the house. Harlan was back, too, and he called to her from the kitchen.

"Get in here. I have some hot chocolate for you."

"There is a God," Divinity murmured as she sat down at the kitchen table.

"I still think you could talk with Isaac on the phone."

"Ears are big in a jail, and some of the details I'd rather not share with someone who might go running to the prosecutor."

Harlan frowned. "Can't see anybody around here running to see Garret. Looks down his nose at most folks."

She smiled, then watched the houseman for a moment.

"What? You got something on your mind, spit it out, Divinity."

"Harlan, have you ever heard about a group of people who play hunting games?"

Frowning, Harlan stirred a cauldron of soup big enough to bathe in. "Everybody in the county's heard one thing or another. A while back some no-accounts were going after coyotes and coy dogs." At her questioning look he explained. "Coyotes mate with local dogs. Their issue are called coy dogs. Most old-timers think we've got so many coyotes now, they don't bother with the local dogs."

"Oh."

"Where was I? Oh. The fools got into the habit of stalking them and shooting them. The sheriff put the word out that if it wasn't stopped, he'd jail every person hanging out on the islands and confiscate their guns. It stopped. None of the ones involved have a lick of sense. Mouths much bigger than their brains. They had a place over on the Iron Bridge Road, but it burned down . . ." He looked pensive.

"What?"

"An out-of-town girl was found dead near there. Forgot all about that."

"Janis Wismer?"

He shook his head. "Nope. She was local. This one

was from out of state, I think. Didn't seem to have family."

"What happened to her?"

"Got drunk. Walked into traffic on the thruway. Hit-and-run. This have something to do with Isaac?"

"It could. LeRoy Wilkins has a body in his lab. The girl's name is Wendy Laidlaw, supposedly a victim of a hit-and-run."

"There's more. I can see it on your face, but you'd rather not discuss it."

"As soon as I know if what I plan works, I'll tell you. Fair enough?"

"Yep. I'll help all I can."

"Thanks." She lifted her cup. "This was great." She rose to her feet. "Better get to work."

"You go ahead. I'll bring another cup along in a bit."

"Thank you." She was almost to the door when she remembered something. "Harlan, who are Willie and Lithcomb?"

"Willie Tarker. She flies the rescue helicopter for the county. Lithcomb is her brother. He and their other two brothers, Milford and Horace, run a security company out of Geneva. Sometimes they've done guard work for Jake. He's using them on the site now since he had the break-in."

"Oh."

"Ex-Marines, all of 'em." He scowled. "You think we need 'em here?"

"No. Jake mentioned he wanted Lithcomb to watch Linnie."

"He would. Lithcomb's sweet on her. If Jake feels it's necessary, he'll have 'em here too."

The back door opened, and a blast of cold wind came from the pantry.

"Close that door, Junior. You'll make my cake fall."

"I did."

Divinity grinned. "How did you know it was Jake, Harlan?"

Harlan rolled his eyes. "Always comes in the same way, like a bull after a heifer." He reddened. "Sorry, Miss Divinity. I know you aren't a country girl."

"True, but I do know what a bull and a heifer are."

Harlan grinned, then turned to look at Jake in the doorway. "Wipe your feet?"

"Yep."

Divinity laughed. "I'll be in the library."

"I'm right behind you," Jake murmured. "Order some hot chocolate."

"He's bringing it."

"You have clout. Someday teach me how you handle Harlan."

She slanted a look at him. "You do pretty well in your own way." It pleased her to see his neck redden. She shouldn't be the only vulnerable one.

He stayed at her side as they walked down the wide corridor leading to the library. "Harlan was on his high horse yesterday about me not keeping the driveway clean. And I should check the roof. Damn! With that pitch I could slide off like a snowball."

"So that's why you didn't linger in the kitchen? You thought he'd land you with more chores."

"Damn right."

Divinity slipped through the library door, hand over her mouth.

"Keep laughing. Just hope he doesn't turn his big guns on you." Jake grimaced. "Wait until spring. He'll have a list of grievances a mile long."

"At least." Divinity chuckled, looking around the library. "This house is bigger than it looks from the outside."

Jake nodded. "It was well constructed when costs were down and the best materials readily available, before the Civil War."

She sat down behind the desk, pushing at the sheaf of notes there, making room for the notebook she always carried with her. Flipping through the pages, she studied them for a moment, then pulled Janis Wismer's journal from her briefcase. She tapped it, looking up at Jake. "I've gone over this a hundred times. It's interesting, but as it stands I'm not sure I could use any of it."

He took the chair opposite her. "We need to find out more about those parties she talks about, the people she met. I'd like to look through it again. If we could connect some of those people to Penny, you might have the ace you need."

She nodded. "We can always hope." She proffered the journal.

Jake put his hand over hers when he reached for it.

"What?" she asked.

"You're doing a good job, Divinity Brown."

"Thanks. I just wish I had more."

"You'll win."

When he looked into her eyes, she had the feeling he saw through to her soul. "You're staring, Jake."

"I am. You're prettier'n any heifer," he said, imitating Harlan's twang, though his tone was husky, sensual.

Her heart missed several beats. She wanted him to kiss her. She wanted to stroke his thick hair.

He stared down at her hand, turning it over, then brought it to his mouth. "Maybe you think you came to Yokapa County to veg out, Divinity. I think you were sent to help Isaac." He kissed her palm. "And save me."

Divinity tried to breathe. She couldn't, feeling dizzy at the cluster of emotions that besieged her. "All—all in a day's work."

"Except you've taken some extra steps. I can see it in Isaac. He's gotten his spirit back." His smile was crooked. "And you've done a great job on me. Ask Harlan."

She swallowed. She couldn't answer that without getting teary, so she concentrated on Isaac. "I wish I could be sure of the case. There's an avalanche of material against Isaac."

Jake nodded, his tender smile said he understood the change of topic. "LeRoy's testimony will bolster you. The journal could help." He leaned forward on the desk. "You know you've turned my life upside down."

"Oh." Air wheezed up her throat. She wanted him. He was nice, and so damned sexy. They stared at each other for lost moments.

"Divinity . . ." He stretched farther and gave her a hard kiss.

"What?" The question came out in two syllables.

"I like your name." He drew in a shuddering breath, then took the journal and left.

"I like yours, Jake," she whispered. She put her hand over her eyes. "I'm still swimming in quicksand, but my stroke's improving." She groaned and picked up her notes.

Divinity had Harlan bring her dinner to the library, not wanting to lose any work time. An hour later Jake appeared in the doorway. "How's it going?"

"I'm putting some things together. How about you?" She pointed her pen at the journal he was holding. "How many times have you read it?"

"Quite a few. I'm picking up things I missed the first time. Pretty revealing. I might know more of the people than I first thought."

"Could we question them?"

"I doubt it. The ones I know wouldn't be classified as friends. Some I dislike as much as they do me."

Divinity sat back in the swivel chair. "There's more."

He nodded. "Some of them are on the list you showed me of witnesses submitted by the prosecution."

She rummaged through her desk and angled a list his way. He showed her the list of names he'd made, then sat down to compare the lists.

"I saw the name Forcer mentioned over and over

again in the journal," she said. "Do you know who that is?"

Jake shook his head. "I wondered about that one. Whoever it is seems to be the head honcho with the 'games' group. Probably has more than a hat size IQ."

Divinity nodded. "Could it be someone named Force or La Force?"

"Could be. I don't recognize it." He looked at his watch, then leaned across the desk and picked up the phone, dialing. "Hello, Linnie? It's Jake."

Divinity listened while Jake questioned Linnie about Forcer. He hung up, shaking his head. "She doesn't know."

"I wish I did. I'd like to talk to this person and get some answers about this group. Janis Wismer mentions him many times in relation to the group. I got the feeling she wasn't too close to him, or didn't know much about him."

"She might've been afraid of him." Jake leaned back in his chair, balancing on the back legs. Even when Divinity was worried, she had a serene beauty that made his mouth go dry. "I don't know that finding the one called Forcer would work for you. He probably wouldn't answer any questions because you represent authority. Most of the guys that I know who hang with this group have done time for one thing or another. They don't like the law that much."

"He might know what happened to Janis Wismer and Penny Elgin-Brown, the Laidlaw and Lynch women, and be willing to talk about it."

"Maybe. I doubt it. Those river rats stick together.

From what some of the men who work for me tell me, most of those guys are bar stool bums with no steady employment. They're not much, but they're loyal to their own kind. Most of the time." He scowled. "Besides, I wouldn't want you talking to them. I'd rather let some guys on my crew sound them out."

"I hope they can." She put the journal in the center desk drawer and locked it.

Jake leaned forward. "Stay cool. You're doing a good job."

Divinity steepled her hands to still their shaking. He was really getting to her. Sexy, handsome, and kind. A wild combination. "The second day of the hearing's tomorrow. We've gotten more information and"—she pushed at a stack of paper—"a list of witnesses who are mostly character witnesses. I'd be happy if we had more solid evidence clearing Isaac." She jumped to her feet. "I've gone over and over my notes. I wish I didn't see so many holes." She stared out the window at the snow heaped on the terrace. "I think we can prove reasonable doubt which is what we need to do. I'd feel better if I knew more about the mysterious Forcer." Her mouth twisted. "A formidable name. It conjures up hairy-chested behemoths."

Jake walked up behind her, his arms sliding around her waist. "You're getting there. Don't doubt yourself. I can tell you Isaac has as much faith in you as I do."

She turned in his arms, her forehead pressed against his chest. "That helps more than you know."

He lifted her chin, letting his mouth settle over

hers. The kiss went on and on, as they took and gave solace, emotion, and a growing heat.

When the phone rang neither moved for a moment. The sound seemed to come from another planet.

"I'll pull the damn thing out of the wall," Jake finally muttered against her lips.

Divinity gulped air. "Have to answer."

"I know." He kissed her again, his tongue touching hers. Then he strode from the room.

Divinity swallowed and tried to breathe evenly. "Hello?" she said into the phone.

"Divi, it's Des. How are you?"

It took her a moment to orient herself, to remember her friend Destiny Smith, and reply. Jake was so large in her mind, he all but blotted out anything else. "Des! Where are you? I haven't heard from you in ages. When I tried to call before I moved up here, I kept getting your machine. So I left a message where I'd be and the number. Are you all right?"

"Fine . . . in a way."

"Meaning?"

"Racer and I are divorced. I got the final papers. It's what we both wanted. End of discussion."

"I see. I'm sorry. I was hoping it would turn around. You seemed so right for each other."

"We aren't. When I see you, I'll go into more detail. Too complicated for a phone call."

"Oh? Are you sure you're all right?"

"Yes, but I've had my moments. Retreating to the country, as you have, has become more appealing. I've begun to see why you buried yourself. What are you up to?"

"Ah . . . I'm on a case—"

"What? I don't believe it."

"Believe it." Divinity paused. "And you might be able to help. Remember those antigovernment groups you dealt with when you were with the Bureau?"

"I've given up government work, Divi. I'm thinking of opening my own private investigating business."

"Are you serious?"

"I am." There was a long pause. "About those antigovernment groups, Divi, be careful with people like that. Some of them are more dangerous than they seem. They resemble those Nazi toughs during the Hitler years. Remember helping me research that? I did my doctoral thesis on those scoundrels." She sighed. "I should've stayed with teaching history at Mill Valley College. It was less chaotic."

"I recall how your days and nights ran together for quite a while."

"Right. I can tell you there are some very nasty people in our country. Some are visible, others masquerade as do-gooders, hiding their violence behind law and order. You know, Mom, Apple Pie, and Family, and keep your guns trained on everyone who disagrees with you. Don't mess with them, Divinity."

"I might have already. I don't know. Could you send me some names, places, information about this area? I have a feeling this case might involve a clubby group addicted to violence against women. I'm not sure. Oh, have you ever heard the name Forcer when you were doing work along those lines?"

"Doesn't ring a bell, but I'll go through my files."

"I'd appreciate it." She went on to tell her friend about Isaac and the case.

"Be careful, Divinity. I don't like the sound of it."

"I will."

"Other than this Forcer and his people, what else is worrying you?"

Divinity chuckled. "Still sharp, I see."

"Actually I'm sharper than I ever was."

Divinity leaned back in her chair. "You make me feel better."

"Good. What's the rest of it?"

Divinity considered telling her friend about Jake, but decided against it. It was too new, too tenuous. They talked awhile longer, and though the conversation wasn't exactly soothing, Divinity felt a certain comfort when she hung up.

She worked long into the night. Jake came in to say something to her, but she was too caught up in what she was doing to pay attention. After midnight she fell into bed and a dreamless sleep.

The phone rang the next morning just before Divinity's alarm went off at six. It was the clerk at the courthouse calling to tell her the hearing had been postponed due to snow. Nearly a foot had fallen overnight. Divinity wasn't sure if she was glad or sad. Sometimes the waiting was the worst.

Harlan greeted her as she entered the kitchen and handed her a glass of freshly squeezed orange juice.

"You're putting in a lot of hours, at the jail and in the library," he said. "Sit down. I have oatmeal for you, raisin toast, and grapefruit. Maybe it's just as well that the judge called off the hearing today. Plows are out, but there's whiteouts all along the highway."

Divinity nodded. "Not everyone would be able to get through the snow."

He pushed a bowl of diced ruby grapefruit toward her as she seated herself at the breakfast bar. "You'll need all the vitamins you can get to face Sandy Garret again."

"I agree." She munched on the tart-sweet fruit, then eyed the assortment of pills Harlan was laying out. "Vitamins?"

"Right." He pointed. "A, K, E, and C." He stabbed at a cylindrical bottle. "That's an herbal mix. Fights off colds and fatigue."

"Oh." She'd rarely taken anything. Under Harlan's watchful eye, she took the lot. "Something new that goes with leasing?"

Harlan scowled. "Tough job ahead of you. You'll need your strength."

They both heard a clatter on the stairs, then Jake entered the kitchen fresh from the shower, his hair still wet. He smothered a yawn and headed for the juice.

"You gonna hang around those joints until you're an old man?" Harlan asked, glaring as he poured Jake a mug of coffee.

Jake couldn't douse the next yawn. He glanced at

Divinity. "Sorry. Didn't get in until late. I was at Danny's."

"Testing the Harley again?" she asked.

He shook his head and tossed back the juice. "Talking to the boys about the vandalism at the site and other things." He cupped his hands around his coffee mug and took the stool next to Divinity. "Everybody has an opinion about the river rats."

Harlan grimaced. "You mean those Sunday cowboys, the ones I was talking about to Miss Divinity yesterday? You think they're dangerous?" Harlan looked both incredulous and appalled. "If they are, we should run them out of this county."

Jake nodded, pouring more juice. "Right." When Harlan dished out some oatmeal for him, he seemed startled. "Even a year ago I would've said we didn't have people like that in this area. I don't think that anymore. Some of the good old boys are getting downright bad."

"What's that mean?" Harlan asked.

Jake glanced at Divinity. "It seems the river rats have played nasty games for some time. Some people have gotten hurt, or punished, as they put it."

"Like murder?" Divinity whispered.

Jake shook his head. "Nobody said that. They skimmed around it, but didn't come out with it."

"Scary," she said.

"Yes. I didn't push by asking questions. I figured they'd clam up fast."

"They would," Harlan said, his lips pursing. "Jackasses. Lumped together I'll bet those bar benders' brains wouldn't add up to a penny."

"And every one of them knows how to use his fists, his rifle, and various assault weapons, according to Butch and Darnell. They're going to keep at it, see if they can find out more."

They finished their breakfasts, then Jake pushed his bowl away. "Want to take a walk?" he asked Divinity.

She thought of the work she could get done with her one-day reprieve. "How about a rain check? Say, later in the day?"

"Done."

"Dinner's ready to microwave when you need it this evening," Harlan said from across the kitchen. "Tonight's my bowling night. I'll be leaving early."

"What about the snow?" Jake asked.

"It'll be clear by then. Never mind me. You two be careful out there. Ain't spring yet."

"I'll take care of her," Jake murmured, enfolding her hand in his.

For the first time in memory Divinity felt totally secure.

# SEVEN

"Are you ready?"

"I was born ready," Sandy said, ignoring Elliot Cranston's frown.

Cranston paced, then paused, drumming his fingers on the icy picnic table.

"Elliot, I told you when you called that I don't like this. It smacks of the illegal. You've heard of coercion. I'm the DA. I don't want anything besmirching this case, or me. If the hue and cry goes up about corruption, the case is blown. Do you want that?"

"You know I don't."

"Then stop this. Stop calling, stop wanting to meet with me."

"I'm worried."

"That's natural. Your son was a friend to the girl—"

"Nothing more."

Sandy took a deep breath, fighting irritation. "You

know I play it straight. I'm sure we have the right man. Stop worrying. I wouldn't even be here if you weren't a member of the club."

"It's not illegal for a father to be concerned about his son," Cranston said, his face reddening. "He's out with those wild friends of his right now, I suppose. I don't like that. Robby is going to have a future."

"I told you not to fret. Robby's not in any trouble. We have the man who committed the crime." Sandy watched the concern on the other man's face fade, but not disappear entirely. "Don't you believe in your son? In the evidence we've gathered to convict Meistersaenger?"

"Of course I do," Cranston all but shouted, then he looked around, eyes narrowed. Though they were very near the park's parking lot, a copse of pine trees hid them from prying eyes. No one was around. He'd made sure of that before Garret's arrival. "I don't like it. At the time of the—the killing, Robby was in the vicinity. He'd just been in her company, when that—that—"

"Whore?"

"I don't call her that." Cranston glared at Sandy. "The morals of males and females are looser than they were when I was young. It's a different world. I don't say I approve of the free and easy ways of young people today, but I keep most of my opinions to myself. I've been a conservative all my life, lived that way, voted the same. Young people look on sex and life in general as a game anybody can play. They experiment with it, with drugs, and anything else that comes their way.

With all they know about communicable diseases it shouldn't be that way, but it is." He struck his hand with his fist. "We shouldn't even be having this problem, let alone this conversation, and not just because of the legality. Robby and his friends are too careless. I don't approve of the new solutions either, abortion and such."

"Abortion isn't new. It's been going on for—"

Cranston waved his hand, interrupting. "I know, I know. I just can't accept the way some people view things today, but I don't look down on all of them." He exhaled, his breath clouding in the cold. "I don't like it that she died, or that Robby knew her . . . so well."

Sandy shook his head. "That's not a crime. I'm a conservative thinker myself, you know that. You're my friend. I know you're very upright and moral. So is your son. The defense will try to make Robby look guilty because he knew her, and because they want to whitewash Isaac Meistersaenger. I don't intend to let it happen because Meistersaenger is guilty and he should be in prison. I'm damned sure I can prove my case against him. And once the jury studies the evidence, he'll be incarcerated. If I wasn't sure of that, I would have given this case to someone else." He smiled when he saw Cranston's face sag in relief. "We'll get the job done. Robby will be back home doing whatever it is he does, and all will be well."

Cranston nodded. "I hope to God you're right."

"I know I am. Now let's get out of here. It's freezing."

Cranston watched Sandy drive away, somewhat mollified, even if a voice deep inside him told him there was still danger to his son. He had every intention of seeing to it that Robby was never connected to the crime. No way would he let Robby be sent to prison. He was going to medical school.

There was still some daylight when Jake and Divinity met for their walk. Divinity clutched his hand as they strolled along. "How do you feel about a microwave meal tonight?"

Jake smiled. "Have to settle, I guess. That's Harlan's truck pulling out now."

"So we're alone."

He looked at her, nodding.

Divinity reached up and pulled his head down. Their mouths met, their tongues touching. Fire licked through her from toe to crown. Never had she felt such power, and such weakness.

Jake tore his mouth from hers. "Divinity," he murmured, running his mouth up and down her jaw. "I need you."

Taking deep breaths, she leaned back and nodded. "We could eat first. Then again, we could make love and then eat. What's your choice?"

"You have to ask?"

His throaty answer had her shivering. "The same as mine then."

"Do you mind if I carry you into the house?"

"No." When he lifted her, she buried her face in

his neck, sighing with joy that he was holding her. She helped him open the outer door, both of them laughing as though there was some joke, instead of just pure happiness.

"It came so fast," she said.

"Miracles are like that," he answered, his tone hoarse.

He carried her to the stairs, stopping on each one to kiss her. In his room he yanked back the covers with one hand, then lowered the two of them to the bed. "You're everything that's wonderful, that works, on this planet, Divinity. I just thought you should know."

She gulped. Such simple words, adorned with emotion only. She wanted to tell him so much, yet she didn't know how. Pulling his face down to hers, she kissed him, openmouthed, wanting. Never had she needed the *solace* of lovemaking. Physical desire, the soothing of the spirit that sexual bonding could bring had all been part of her life in short spans. She'd never been shaken to her soul with the kind of searing need gripping her now. She could forget today, tomorrow, yesterday. There was only the moment and the beautiful *comfort* of rising passion. She needed it, and Jake. She reached for him and held on tight.

"Oh, baby," he said, "you don't know what you're doing to me."

"Do too," she whispered, gripping him harder. "I want you."

He leaned back from her, eyes lazy and fire filled. "Did I tell you that I made a promise to my dead mama that the next time I did the sex thing, I'd do the honorable deed and marry the lady?"

"Bull."

"No. I mean it." The lazy smile toughened just a hair. "I'd like you to want it too." Before she could answer, his mouth was on hers again, taking and giving, building an inferno that surrounded them and wouldn't free them. Hunger roared through them. There was no thought of denial. There was only a mounting need that cascaded over and around them.

Divinity arched against him, seeking his heat, her arms sliding up and around his neck, locking there.

In moments their clothing was discarded and they were skin-to-skin.

His fingers slid over her soft, curving breasts, pressing, caressing.

She whispered his name, asking, praying for . . . what?

Responding as though she'd shouted, he rose onto his knees and pulled her up until she was taller than he, her nipples fitting easily between his lips.

As the sucking began she quivered, hands stroking his thick hair, coaxing, desiring more. The keening sound coming from her was a demand, and he gave, taking her more fully into his mouth. The way she gripped him excited his fervor, her legs moving against his lower body and thighs.

When he released her, their breathing was ragged, their gazes locked. He let her slide down and took her mouth, his tongue tasting her as she tasted him. As though the jousting with mouths took them beyond permission or question, they leaned back and stared at each other.

"We might be a tad past casual," she told him. She touched his hard jaw, noting the resolve, the tough set of his mouth. "I don't relish being one of your women."

"I don't want to be just one of your men."

She choked on a laugh. "This might be one of the stupidest things I've done." She was ensnared in the hottest, most sexual moment of her life. Still she needed to qualify, to build any type of barrier against hurt. If she warned herself, if she readied herself for what might occur, if there was some armor . . .

He put his forehead against hers. "Then again it might be the best thing you've ever done." He kissed her forehead. "We've had this conversation before. I thought we settled things."

"We did."

"Then let's not miss our chance. It might be all we'll get."

She put her arms around his neck.

Jake saw the sheen of tears in her eyes, how her smile trembled. He felt a similar agony to her soul-searching, yet also a surety that this was right for all time, no matter how uncertain the rest of his life might be. "You call the shots, Divinity." He leaned down and kissed her between the breasts, then lifted his mouth to hers. "Of course, if you call this off, I'm filling the hot tub with ice cubes and moving there."

She took his hand, bringing it to her cheek. "Love me, Jake."

"Yes."

His hands skimmed over her breasts until her nipples became so sensitized, she thought she'd scream. Their bodies seemed hinged together as they moved on the bed. Just a touch set off a fire. His kisses took away her worry, her concern. She needed the passion, if only for a moment, but she knew she desired it for a lifetime.

Jake took his time loving her. Divinity was a feast of beauty, and he needed it. He moved down her body, his tongue darting to her navel, his mouth skimming across her ribs. She arched like a bow when his tongue touched her woman's core. Grasping his head, she hauled him upward. "I—I can't. I'm too . . . too . . ."

Jake groaned, and without hesitation, he entered her.

She took him and held him. He was hard and full. She was moist and snug. He looked down into her face, sweet with passion, her lips parting on short, quick puffs of air. Feeling hotter and more needful than ever before, he pushed deeper into her. Her eyes widened. "Lord, Divinity, you are some kind of wonderful."

"So are you."

He moved, holding himself back with supreme effort. When she raised her hips to meet his smooth thrusts, he groaned again.

Each motion took her breath, but she needed him

so badly, she couldn't deny herself. As she began the climb, he held her steady, letting his own passion escalate in concert with her. Taking her mouth, he pushed harder into a headier pace, one that soon overwhelmed them. Long and strong, the ripples of passion turned into cascades convulsing their bodies. With it came a balming fire that forged them, carrying them past uncertainty into a blazing acceptance.

Neither moved for a thousand heartbeats. Still connected, Jake looked at her. "Great casual sex, Madame Attorney."

"Yes. I thought it should get high marks."

"Very." He kissed her ear. "How about a shower?"

She nodded, and he edged away from her, groaning. He wanted her again! That instant.

He dropped back to her again. "I want you already."

"Wow." She whistled the word, almost grabbing for him. "Let's get under the shower," she said instead.

He led her to the large glass-bricked enclosure, and warm water soon coursed over them.

"I don't want to depend on anyone too much," she said abruptly. "You've become a bulwark. I don't know if I want to handle that . . . or if I can."

He grinned. "Then think of me as your stud of the month."

"Stud of the month?" She laughed, then choked when she swallowed water. "Jake . . . Blessing . . . that's . . . awful," she said, laughing and coughing at the same time.

"No, it isn't. Being your stud of the month is a coup for me."

"How's that?" She grabbed a loofah sponge and began washing him.

"Because . . . because . . . Damn, you've made me hot again. He flipped off the water, draped bath sheets over them, and ran with her for the bed.

Her laughter faded in the unrelenting emotion that overwhelmed her.

Lord, she prayed. Don't let him be too good to be true.

The next day, Valentine's Day, the hearing resumed. Sandy Garret presented more evidence, then it was Divinity's turn.

She squeezed Isaac's arm and rose to her feet. "Your Honor, in order for a trial to take place, there has to be hard evidence. Though the prosecution has built a plateau of probabilities, it has yet to come up with a shred of solid evidentiary material that would link my client to the crime."

Divinity then called LeRoy to the stand and had him tell the court what he had told her and Jake. He explained how he happened to have Wendy Laidlaw's body; how both she and Penny Elgin-Brown had been strangled to death; how beneath their fingernails appeared to have been scraped clean, but that he and the ME had found enough tissue for LeRoy to test for DNA. Finally, he testified that the DNA from the tissue found on both girls matched, and that although it was similar to Isaac's, it was not the same as his.

The muted uproar when he finished was enough to keep the judge's gavel pounding for nearly a minute.

Sandy Garret tried to shake LeRoy with his own questioning, but LeRoy was an experienced expert witness and refused to budge from his testimony. When the hearing recessed for the day, Divinity finally felt there was a good chance the case would never go to trial.

The next day was the last day of the hearing. Divinity called her character witnesses to the stand, then she and the DA made their final arguments to the judge. He declared the hearing over and said he would give his judgment in two days, on Friday.

They all rose as he left the courtroom, then Divinity turned to Isaac. She was taken aback when he smiled.

"You were good, Divinity Brown," he said. "You struck like an avenging angel and took my fear away."

She patted his shoulder. "Be strong. You're innocent."

He nodded and went with his guards. Sighing, she started pushing her scattered notes into her briefcase.

"If I'm ever in a fight, I want you at my back," Jake said behind her.

She turned. "I've got a good left hook. My father taught me."

Jake looked into her eyes. "It was rough today, but you didn't give ground. You were damned convincing."

She bit her lip. "I had to be. I can't let him down. I'd swear on ten Bibles he was innocent."

"And you would've given him the same tough defense had you thought otherwise."

"It's my job."

He took her arm. "It's going to be all right."

"It's up to the judge." She sighed again. "It's going to be tough on Isaac if we go to trial."

"I think you punched some big holes in the prosecution's case when LeRoy took the stand." He leaned down and kissed her cheek. "The judge will decide against the prosecution."

Divinity's heart beat out of rhythm. She couldn't help but love him. "And how do you know this, oh great wise one?"

"Because there's a dance Saturday night at the country club, the traditional Hunt Club Ball that raises money for charity." He grinned. "Nobody would come if this weren't settled." He sobered. "It's going to work all around."

Divinity straightened. "I have to believe it."

"Do . . . and then tell me you'll come to the ball with me."

She smiled. When he took her hand, she clutched his. He had become her anchor. She needed his touch, his confidence.

Friday morning came too fast, yet not fast enough. Divinity smiled at Isaac when they rose to greet the judge, hoping her nervousness didn't show.

The judge looked at them, then cleared his throat. "I don't find there is enough true evidence to remand Isaac Meistersaenger over for trial." A wisp of a smile crossed his face. "In other words, Isaac Meistersaenger is free to go."

The courtroom was in an uproar. Divinity hugged Isaac, not even attempting to speak over the din.

Isaac and his family thanked her profusely.

"God will bless you, Divinity Brown," Ephraim said to her.

"Thank you."

Her heart was so full, she couldn't speak to Jake when he approached, putting his arm around her.

"You're wonderful," he said. "I'm taking you out to celebrate, lady, just the two of us."

"Yes, please."

After they'd eaten lunch at the town's best restaurant, Divinity was still on a high. Justice had triumphed. For the first time in weeks she could relax. She toyed with the idea of calling LeRoy Wilkins and thanking him again. If he hadn't been such a solid witness, they might very well be preparing for a trial now.

"What would you like to do?" Jake asked as they entered The Arbor. He looked at her suggestively. "Harlan's not here."

She smiled, tempted by the idea of spending the afternoon in bed with Jake. "Let's go see LeRoy," she said impulsively. "Without him, we probably wouldn't be celebrating today. I'd like to thank him in person."

"Let's go then."

The door creaked open to LeRoy Wilkins's lab. He didn't notice because he was too deep into what he was doing. He knew Isaac had been released for lack of evidence, but there were still many questions. He'd become intrigued by them, and one of them held him in thrall at that moment.

Something jarred his consciousness—an unusual sound perhaps—and he realized he wasn't alone. He heard footsteps, bare whispers against the wood, and he realized his unexpected visitor might be trouble. He pushed the paper he was filling with names and stats to the edge of the desk, letting it flutter to the floor. It couldn't be seen unless someone went around his chair.

"Come out, whoever you are," he called. "There's nothing to steal here."

"There might be."

The voice was disguised. Why? "Look for yourself."

"I intend to."

He needed to hear more. There was something cultured in the rough intonations. "If you tell me what you want, I can get it for you."

"I can get it myself."

LeRoy figured he was going to be killed. The bastard would get nothing from him. "I have an elaborate filing system. If you just tell me what it is—"

"Shut up."

"Of course." LeRoy's hand inched toward his desk lamp. "I was only trying to help."

"No, you weren't. You're trying to stall."

"Nonsense." LeRoy swept the lamp from the desk, trying to throw himself sideways at the same time. A blinding pain erupted in his left hand. He yelled.

A karate chop struck his neck, knocking him to the floor.

"Fool."

# EIGHT

"What?" Jake asked, his eyes on the road.

Divinity blinked and looked out the windshield, pretending she hadn't been staring at him for the past few minutes. "I didn't say anything."

"Not with your lips. Your eyes were talking."

"Oh? And they were saying?"

"Asking questions about me, whether I'd be a great husband, a great father, a great provider—"

"Hold it. I thought we settled this."

"We did, but I was reading questions in your look."

Behind his smile she saw the uncertainty that she'd lived with for a long time. "I would've said when we first met that we weren't anything alike. Now I realize we're very similar in some ways."

"You mean like not believing I could be lucky enough to have a woman like you."

She reached over the console to put her hand on

his leg. "No, like not believing my luck in finding a man like you."

Jake groaned, pulling around a slower vehicle on Route 96. "I wish we weren't going to LeRoy's. I'd rather take you to bed."

"Aha, you had one of those 'hot sheet' places on the highway in mind."

Laughing, he shook his head. "Divinity Brown, you can be bad."

"I can," she said in a sultry tone, running her finger up his arm, then leaning over to kiss his cheek.

"Don't! Even the smallest kiss from you blows me apart."

"Ahh, my plan is working. I've every intention of seducing you."

"Lord, I don't need this. LeRoy is causing me a lot of pain."

"Poor man." She kissed his ear.

"We might not get there," Jake said through his teeth. "I have a condo on Seneca Lake that's getting closer."

"Can't. I want to see LeRoy."

He grinned. "You've gotten playful since you won Isaac's case."

"Technically I didn't *win*."

"Getting thrown out is the same as winning." He glanced at her. "I'm proud of you."

She swallowed, words sticking in her throat. "It's a great feeling to do the right thing, isn't it?" she managed to say at last. "The look on Isaac's face will stay with me for a long time."

"Yeah."

Lost in the warmth of their love, they didn't need to speak.

When Jake steered into the parking lot of the old county buildings, neither wanted to pierce their wonderful aura by moving.

Jake finally leaned over and kissed her. "I love you."

She cupped his jaw. "I'm so glad."

He hopped out of the truck and went around to her side, opening the door and lifting her out. He kept his arm around her as they walked across the icy tarmac to the building.

Still caught up in the joy of her victory and of Jake's love, Divinity didn't notice when Jake stiffened. She did notice when he stopped walking and muttered a curse.

"What?" she asked.

He nodded to the wide double doors to LeRoy's lab. One was ajar.

"Oh," she said. "LeRoy probably just didn't shut the door all the way. Or maybe the wind . . ." Her voice trailed off at Jake's expression.

"LeRoy wouldn't be so careless," he said, his voice low and taut, "and there's no wind today. Go back to the truck, Divinity."

"No." Curling her purse strap around her hand, she wielded the well-filled bag. "I'm at your back."

His smile twisted, but he said no more. Holding her hand, he pushed the door open and eased inside. No lights! Another warning. LeRoy always had his work area well lit. Cursing that Divinity was behind him and not safe at The Arbor, Jake angled around a tall case and squinted toward where LeRoy's desk was.

They heard the groan at the same time. "Call the sheriff from the truck," Jake ordered.

"No, I'm staying with you," she said, though her voice shook.

Jake rounded the last high bookcase adjacent to LeRoy's desk and went down on his hands and knees. He didn't see LeRoy, he felt him. He leaned over his friend, bracing his head, putting his mouth to his ear. "Is he still here?"

"I think he left," LeRoy said in a louder, quavery voice.

"Help's on the way. Divinity—"

"I'm right here. I'll try to find the phone."

"Wait." Jake pulled off his jacket and used it to cushion LeRoy's head. "Let me find the light."

He felt for the switch, then flipped it on. The sudden light had him blinking, then he sank to his knees next to LeRoy. "Take it easy, man. Who did this?"

LeRoy licked his lips. "Thirsty."

Divinity went to the water fountain on the wall, filling a paper cup. She brought it back to Jake, then went to the phone to call 911. After giving the necessary information to the operator, she doused some paper towels in cold water and put them on LeRoy's head.

"Don't cry, Divinity," he said, his voice raw.

"I'm so . . . so sorry."

"Who did it, LeRoy?" Jake asked.

LeRoy tried to shake his head, wincing with pain when he did. He closed his eyes for a moment, sighing. "Don't know, Jake. Tried to keep him talking."

Divinity shushed him, telling him to lie still. "You might have a concussion. Please don't move."

"Hurts," LeRoy whispered.

"You didn't see him?"

"Jake! He shouldn't talk."

"Sorry. Blink your eyes, LeRoy."

LeRoy's chuckle was stopped by his groan.

"Stop it, Jake."

"Sorry." He looked past Divinity, talking to himself. "I don't think he knows who hit him." Jake didn't seem to see Divinity shake her head. "Whoever it was knew how to hurt." When she looked puzzled, he pointed to LeRoy's left hand and leaned close to her ear. "Broke his fingers."

She gasped. "Monster."

"Meant to cause pain," LeRoy managed to say. "All . . . in . . . black, like those guys . . . in . . . James Bond movies." He licked his lips. "Still thirsty." He looked at Jake. "Felt . . . I . . . should . . . know him." Sighing, he slumped against Divinity, even as she was holding the cup to his lips.

"I think he's fainted." Divinity swallowed back her tears. "Could this have happened because I had him testify?" Guilt roared through her. "We shouldn't have asked for his help."

"Don't look at it that way. LeRoy is a talented man who likes to use his gifts."

"But if this is because he testified for Isaac . . ."

Jake shook his head. "I don't think so, Divinity, but the police will check it out. I think some dopehead dropped by to see if he could score with LeRoy's chemicals."

Before she could question him, the police were there, the emergency crew at their heels.

Jake and Divinity hovered behind the medics as they bent over LeRoy.

"How is he?" Jake asked.

"He could be better, Jake," one of them said. "Some sucker really tried to hurt him. Let's go, everybody."

In minutes LeRoy was on a gurney and out the door, tubes in his arms, nose, and mouth.

Jake jogged next to the medic. "He has the best, Lem."

"I hear you, Jake. I'll stay with him all the way."

"Good. I'm going to ask the Tarkers to guard him at the hospital."

"Gotcha, Jake. Let me know what's going on here, will you?"

"Someday. Not now."

Lem saluted, then climbed into the back of the ambulance.

Jake watched the vehicle pull away, a police escort in front of it, then strode back into LeRoy's place. A uniformed man with a potbelly and a nose to match was talking to Divinity.

"Sheriff, how are you?"

The sheriff turned to Jake. "What do you know about this?"

Jake put his arm through Divinity's. "This is Divinity Brown. Divinity, this is Sheriff Lester."

"I introduced myself, Jake," the sheriff said, his tone sandpaper dry. "You trying to fox me or something?"

"Not me."

"Then what's this bull about introducing me so formally to Miss Brown?"

"Just wanted to make sure you knew—"

"Uh-huh." The sheriff waved his arm. "I know who she is and what she does."

"Good. Then you know she's the able lawyer who defended—"

"I know that, too, Jake. I went to the hearing."

Divinity nodded. "Yes, I saw you there when I questioned two of your deputies, Frenzel and Cory."

"Frenzel and Cory. Right. Good men." His smile slipped to Jake. "Well? What went on here? Are you going to tell me or give me another song and dance?"

"I wouldn't do that, Sheriff."

"Sure you would, Jake, but I won't let you."

Jake told him in short, quick sentences what they knew, omitting what LeRoy had said to them.

"I see. I'll want to go into this in more detail, Jake, so keep yourself handy."

"Will do."

The sheriff looked around the room, then walked over to his crime team.

Jake turned to Divinity and noticed her interest in LeRoy's desk. "What?"

"He might've left us something, a message. I don't know."

"He never said anything like that," Jake whispered, his gaze going over the cluttered desk.

"Didn't you say he was a genius?"

"And more." He glanced at the sheriff, then moved closer to LeRoy's desk. "LeRoy is meticulous, though this looks messy. He always knows where everything is on his desktop."

They both inched nearer to the desk. Divinity's attention went from the sheriff to the piles of paper.

"See anything?" Jake didn't look her way, trying to keep her shielded in case the sheriff glanced at them. Just then he did, and Jake smiled. When the sheriff frowned, Jake widened his smile. "Divinity!"

"Wha . . . Oh." She smiled at the sheriff, too, folding her hands in front of her. She stayed that way, until someone called the lawman. "Let's try to look through this stuff," she muttered to Jake.

"He'll probably throw me in jail."

"It's worth it."

"Thank you, Divinity," he said, his tone dry. It was enough for him that she grinned in that special way.

"Let's assume LeRoy was attacked because he testified for the defense. Let's also assume he was taking his investigating into Penny's death further." Jake nodded. That sounded like LeRoy. "So there might be something here that could help point to the person who really did murder Penny."

Jake took one last step to the desk, pretending great interest in the microscope sitting on the far corner.

Glancing into the scope, he studied the slow-moving dances of the magnified amoeba, then he eyed the area around the scope. His glance fell to the floor, and he saw a triangle of paper, sticking out from beneath the beat-up desk. Looking around, he waited a second, bent down as if tying his shoe. He palmed the sheet of paper and slipped it into his jacket, anchoring it with his arm.

"Anything?" Divinity whispered.

He shook his head. "Not sure. I didn't look at it. He might've been throwing it out, or maybe he didn't want the intruder to see it."

"Why LeRoy?"

Her whispered query had pain in it. Jake squeezed her hand. "Whoever did this could consider LeRoy, and his expertise, a threat. He must know I'll be looking for him."

"Jake, don't. Let the police handle it. The culprit is dangerous. I don't want you hurt."

"Thanks. I like hearing you say that."

"Jake, listen to me. We have no idea . . ." Her voice trailed off as the sheriff looked over his shoulder at them.

"You still here, Jake?"

"Looks like."

"You have something else to tell me?"

"No, I've told you all I know."

The sheriff's crocodile smile made his bulbous nose quiver. "And you, Miss Brown, you got anything else to say to me?"

"No, sir. As an officer of the court I'm bound to

give you all the information I can that would bring about a just resolution to a problem. I wish I knew more."

The sheriff studied her for a moment, then he looked at Jake again. "Get in touch with me if you think of anything, Jake."

"I will." Jake took hold of Divinity's arm, angling her toward the exit.

"I might need to talk to you again, Jake, and to you, Miss Brown."

"We'll be around, Sheriff," Jake said, and ushered her out the door. "Funny thing," he said. "I've never been one of Sheriff Lester's favorites."

Divinity chuckled, glad he was holding her hand. Night had fallen while they'd been inside. Wispy clouds covered the sky, shutting out the stars, but not the ethereal light of the full moon. For a flash in time Divinity felt the need to wish upon a star, and there wasn't one. For some reason that made her shiver.

Jake drove out of the parking lot, handing her the paper he'd lifted from the floor, then calling Horace Tarker on his car phone. He set it up for Horace and his brothers to watch LeRoy round the clock.

"Anything interesting?" he asked Divinity when he was done. He turned on the interior light so she could see.

"It's just a list of names. Wait a minute. I recognize a lot of these names. It looks like everyone in either law enforcement or the DA's office is on here. At the top are Penny's and Wendy Laidlaw's names, followed by some numbers. It almost looks like he was doing DNA comparisons. But how could he?"

"I don't know. LeRoy has a very convoluted genius. I told you he's a detail man. A year ago we had a bad flu epidemic. Blood samples were taken of a good share of the county. I'm sure LeRoy kept the samples. Not much escapes him."

Divinity sat back, her mind racing. "Do you think he suspected someone in law enforcement, that one of them could've been involved with the murder?"

"Truthfully, LeRoy would suspect his own mother if the facts pointed that way. LeRoy is, and will be until he dies, a man of pure science. He's never been that impressed with the humanity around him, or what it had to offer. He has a way of peeling away the outer skin and getting to the heart of a matter." Jake took the lake road, checking the rearview mirror more often than he usually did.

"You're worried."

"I am."

"Because of LeRoy?"

"Primarily. Also who ever murdered Penny Elgin-Brown hasn't been caught. If he's been at the hearing, or he read this evening's paper, he knows Isaac's been released. If that angers him, or if he decides he wants to commit another crime, no woman in this area is safe. I'm keeping you in close sight until this is settled, one way or the other."

"Thanks." She closed her eyes for a moment, pondering what Jake had said. "If the perpetrator's smart, and I think he is, he might commit another crime, but not in this area. He won't take the chance of being caught." She shuddered as she pondered the fear a woman would suffer in the clutches of such a person.

Jake reached over and took her hand. "He's not getting you."

She swallowed, grasping his hand tightly.

He only released her when he had to turn or shift, then his hand would come right back to hers. As he turned into the driveway to The Arbor, she said, "You handle people well."

He didn't seem confused by her non sequitor. "Not you. You still haven't said you'll marry me."

She didn't look at him. Instead she opened her door and exited the truck. "Do you think spring will come early this year?"

"We'll talk about the weather another time. I want to talk about you, about us."

When he pulled her into his arms, she didn't resist. "Jake, it's happened so fast."

"Sometimes good things do."

She nodded, her face pressed to his chest. "I don't want anything to damage it."

"It won't. We won't let it."

She looked up at him, kissing his jaw. "I've been thinking about going back to being an attorney full-time."

"Would it bother you to practice in this county? If it does, I'll move my business to wherever you are."

"You'd do that?"

"Yes."

"Even though your home is here, you're rooted here?"

"You're my home, Divinity. One day you'll realize it."

"I think I do now. I know I want you in my life."

That earned her a deep, lasting kiss.

"I want forever, Divinity. You know that. I think we should take some giant steps to make that work."

"What's the first one?"

"Marriage."

"Why don't we live together for a while?"

"Gun-shy?"

"I guess so. My first marriage was a joke. I don't think marriage is anything to make fun of, Jake."

"Neither do I."

"Then what do you think about living together?"

"I'm almost there. One more pair of socks and I'm yours."

"Pretty good price, Blessing."

"You could've had me for no socks."

"Wow, you are a bargain."

"I am, but just for you."

"I'll buy that."

Arms around each other, they went into the house. Harlan had already retired, so they made themselves peanut butter and jelly sandwiches for dinner. Grinning wickedly, Jake suggested they be decadent and eat them in bed.

"Did I tell you this is a seduction meal?" he asked as they entered her room.

"Peanut butter and jelly?" She laughed. "What's so

wildly erotic about peanut butter and jelly?" She smiled at him as he unbuttoned her blouse.

"I lulled you into a false sense of security. You thought we were going to read Dr. Seuss. I knew better."

She felt both aroused and amused. He'd brought so much happiness into her life, and he was slowly making it a part of her being. It awed and frightened her that she could have never met him. She said as much.

"Not a chance," he answered. "You're my fate, lady. I thought you knew that."

"Stupid me."

"Not stupid, just not a believer yet."

"I'm getting there."

He pulled her into his arms. "I love holding you."

"I like it too. Lots."

The room was dark, but the moon painted silver on the walls. Jake held her tighter.

"For so many years," he said, "I thought I could never have a relationship like this, that I couldn't love like this even if I wanted to. You came along and altered every perception in my life, Divinity." He leaned back, his smile crooked. "I'm not sure I could live without you."

His words shook her so, she was sure she couldn't answer.

"Nothing to say?" When he saw the tear, he was appalled. "Divinity! I didn't mean to make you cry."

More tears fell. When he cradled her, trying to soothe her, she pushed at him. "Not sad," she said. "Happy."

"You are? Damn, that's wonderful." When she moved back to loosen her bra, he was there, doing it for her, then turning her so his hands could slide around and cup her breasts. "You're very beautiful, in every way a person should be. You're so good. You're kind and thoughtful. I'll be damned if I understand it, but I find that sexy as hell."

She leaned back against him. "I should be bad. Right?"

"You should be as you are." He removed the rest of her clothes, then his own. "You're the sexiest, most beautiful friend I've ever had, and I love you. I'm crazy about you. Oh, honey, don't cry again."

"Then don't . . . say . . . all those . . . things."

"Sorry." He slid his hands over her naked body, then carried her to the bed. Lying down beside her, he caressed her breasts, his thumbs skimming and circling the peaks while his tongue probed her ear.

He used his teeth on her shoulder, gentle piercing stabs that sent electricity to her toes. "I've had all day to think about this, Divinity."

"I'm afraid it entered my mind a few times even when I was in court."

Her laughter feathered his ear, and he thought he'd explode. Pushing her back to the pillows, he leaned over her. "Stop this, woman. You make me want you too much."

"That's my master plan."

"It's working."

Entranced, she lifted her arm when he caressed it with his tongue. "More."

"There will be," he said against her breasts. "You're not in a hurry, are you?"

"I am . . . but I don't want you to go fast. Very slow."

He groaned. "Your voice is driving me around the bend."

"Great."

He rolled her over, and the feel of him on her bare back was an erotic experience she hadn't counted on, that had her pulsing to a brand-new rhythm. Never had she expected the sensations curling over her, entering her, changing her, tying her to Jake Blessing.

The first time they'd made love had been so great, she'd thought nothing could surpass it. Already the touch of him was making a lie of that. She was more aroused than she'd ever been, and she felt the same response in him. Nothing in her life had prepared her for Jake Blessing. Always she'd been able to plan for what came her way. Jake had wiped out her need to be in control, taken away her assumptions of how she should feel. It was wild, wonderful, and awesome, and she wanted it for all time.

Turning her head, she let his mouth find hers again. Her lips, drenched in a passion so new, so sweet, so needed, clung to his. As though she'd spoken to him, he understood her desire for more. She needed and wanted all of him, not just in the throes of wonderful passion, but at breakfast, lunch, and dinner, and all the times in between. Sensation after cataclysmic sensation rocked her, arching her body, eliciting groans from him when she rubbed against him.

Just his tongue abrading hers, his fingers caught in her hair, his teeth nipping at her sensitized skin, was enough to push her onto the springboard of sexual satisfaction. The ascension was a rocketing ride that took her breath away.

More than the strong body with the iron hardness pressed against her, beyond the blue heat of spiraling passion, was the surety that she could lose all control with Jake Blessing and gain a lifetime of joy.

The delight he gave her boomeranged over him, cascading showers of hot pleasure. His fingers slid down her middle playing her like a beautiful instrument, even as her hands feathered over him.

"Jake?"

"Yes, darling."

"This is too wonderful."

"It is."

"Will we always have it?"

"Beyond the life of our great-great-grandchild."

"Wow."

Voices faded as the rush began.

Gasping at the impact of the wild orgasm that shocked and delighted her, she hurtled into the hot abyss of satisfaction. When she buckled under the onslaught, he didn't release her. He caught her on her side, entering her even as she fell from the first burst of passion.

"Again?" she whispered.

"Oh yes," he said, hoarse and wild with want.

He moved into her with gentle thrusts, pushing her libido into high gear once more. They shook with the heady completeness of sexual rightness, alone and unafraid on the mountaintop.

She'd become part of him, Jake realized, like a platelet in his blood, like tissue connecting his bone, like the air he needed to breathe. Swaying in the maelstrom she loosed in him, he held her.

The more he took of her, the more he needed. It awed him that she gave and gave. Breaths throbbed between them. He explored every inch of her, connected to her, tied to her. Her name shuddered from him again and again.

In the silver moonlight they watched each other as every motion took them higher. Jake pressed deeper and deeper until neither knew where the other began. Frantic gasps filled the air. They clutched each other.

Divinity's eyes flew open when she convulsed around him. She wanted to tell him that she was over the edge, but she couldn't form the words. Hurry! Hurry, come with me! She saw how he flinched, how his eyes fixed to hers. She trembled against him, feeling his answering tremor as they rode the crest higher, and higher. With a burst of rapture they were sucked into the eye of the storm, cast about like leaves in a hurricane. They held each other and inhaled the wonder.

Divinity woke to hear Sting singing an old Gershwin favorite. Had she dropped into another world? She swore she hadn't been asleep, but had been knocked out by Jake's sensual power. She hadn't even felt him leave the bed to put on one of her favorite CDs.

"Hi," he said, snuggling behind her. "You know, I've had less wild rides on a luge sled in the Adirondacks."

"Hmm, something wonderful."

"Isn't it?" He kissed her ear.

She looked over her shoulder at him. "Jake?"

"Hmm?"

"Have you really ridden on a luge?"

His startled laugh had her grinning. "Yes, Divinity, I have. It's great. Would you like to do that?"

"I think I would."

"I'll take you up to the mountains, and we'll do it."

She kissed the side of his hand that curved near her mouth.

"I have a dilemma," he said.

"Only one?"

"Yes. I'm only going to be faithful to you for eighty-one years. After that you either have to decide you'll marry me, or I'm calling off our relationship."

"Impetuous, aren't you?"

"I have to be. I'm forcing a decision out of you."

"Okay. I accept your terms, as long as I have the option of marrying you before the eighty-one years are up."

"Fair enough. I think we should have a contract, all legal and aboveboard. You can handle that."

"Thank you."

"You're welcome. I want you again."

"Good. I was going to mention I was ready."

"Divinity," he groaned, sweeping her around and into his arms.

# NINE

The sun had barely peeped over the horizon the next morning when there was a knock at the back door of The Arbor.

"Good morning, Ephraim Meistersaenger," Harlan said, using the full name as custom required.

"I would speak with Divinity Brown."

Harlan nodded. "She's in the dining room having breakfast with Jake. Come in, please."

Ephraim nodded and followed Harlan through the kitchen to the large dining room.

Divinity set her coffee cup down and smiled at the Amish man. "Good morning."

Ephraim nodded to Jake, then approached her. "You have done God's work, Divinity Brown." He held out a homemade wallet. Divinity took it, seeing that it was filled with ten-dollar bills. She removed what she considered her fee, then handed it back.

Ephraim frowned. "It should be more."

"No, Ephraim Meistersaenger, it shouldn't. The fee is correct." She hesitated. "There is one thing you could do for me, though."

Ephraim inclined his head. "What is it, Divinity Brown?"

"I would like your friendship. I may be settling in this area, and I would be honored to have that."

There was a warmth to Ephraim's look, though he didn't smile. "It is yours." He nodded to Harlan and Jake, then went out the way he came, Harlan at his heels.

Jake smiled. "You have a power, love."

"So have you. Are you ready to go visit LeRoy?"

"Just so long as we don't stay too long. I have to shine my shoes for the big dance tonight."

Divinity laughed, then sobered. "You do think we'll be able to see LeRoy, don't you?"

"Sure. I'll throw my weight around, babe." He pursed his lips. "Of course, that doesn't take into account the Tarker boys. I hope Horace and his brothers let us through." At her chuckle, he grimaced. "You just don't know how tough those guys can be. When they're on the job, they're even worse. Laugh now, but think how bad you'll feel if Lithcomb throws me down the stairs."

"True." She laughed again. Jake had brought so much into her life, not the least of which was the laughter. "You're not just a funny man, Jake, you truly are a blessing. No pun intended." It gave her great satisfaction to see him redden.

"Is that right?"

"Surprised you?"

"Knocked me out." He whipped around the table and pulled her into his arms. "Now that you've crossed your Rubicon, Divinity, why not take it one step further?"

"Which is?"

"Put me out of my misery."

"I can't. No gun."

"That's getting old, Divinity. I just want you to think about it." He led her out of the dining room and down the main hall to the stairs.

"I do, all the time." She stood on the bottom step, her hands on his shoulders, and kissed him. "I'll meet you down here in fifteen minutes."

"Make it five."

It was ten minutes, but he was waiting. They said good-bye to Harlan and left.

"Isaac's case is done, Divinity."

"I know, Jake."

"So take a chance on me." The sun had heated the frosty air. Icicles dripped from the eaves in the barn.

"We're living together."

"And I love that. But I'd like more."

She pressed close to him. "Didn't you get enough last night?" she asked, her voice throaty, her expression teasing.

"None of that," he said, pretending to be stern, although he was grinning. "We're going to see LeRoy, remember?"

"Sure. But I thought maybe we could try out one of those 'hot sheet' places . . ."

He laughed. Pulling her into his arms, he kissed her thoroughly.

Watching them through the binoculars, Robby Cranston ground his teeth.

"Stay cool, Robby boy, we're going to get her. Don't worry."

"I want her torn apart," Robby said, pounding one fist on the steering wheel of the van. "My old man has been all over me since they threw out the case yesterday. In a matter of minutes he cut my allowance in half, and he wants me working full-time under his eye until I go to medical school." Frustrations zinged through him. "All because of her. Why the hell did she have to get him off? He doesn't give a damn about going to jail. He's Amish."

"Whazzat mean, Robby?"

"Shut up. She's jeopardized my freedom. Nobody has a right to do that."

His petulant tone wasn't lost on his passengers. Since they were in the mood for games, they didn't care if Robby had a tantrum. Fun was fun, and Robby Cranston had the money to buy their fun. They would do whatever it took to keep the fountain of funds running.

"That's enough looking, Rob," Dilly Pilato said. "We can get her anytime. Anybody got any stuff?"

"Let's save it until after we take care of the attorney. Then we'll party," Robby said, his voice hard. "We'll take her out at the Hunt Club Ball. Nobody'll miss her for a while. By the time they do, we'll have her out on the river. We'll give her something to make her happy, have some fun with her, then drop her in the river."

"Kill a lawyer? I don't know, Robby."

"Look, Dennis, you want to party, don't you?"

"Yeah, but—"

"No, buts. This is no different than the other times."

"Robby, it's different. This is a lawyer."

"Look, Dilly, you guys want to chicken out, that's fine. When the Forcer finds out that I'm the one who had to do the cleaning up, he won't want you guys around, and there won't be any stuff for you either."

"They're just griping, Robby," Clyde Deering said. "We'll do it, won't we?" Clyde glowered at his companions. They needed Robby to get the stuff. He was their tie-in with the Forcer. "Robby, do you know who the Forcer is? You said you were going to find out."

"Yeah, well, I can't tell you yet." He would have if he knew. He needed to keep his friends in line, and he counted on the drugs to do that. He figured if his source ever dried up, he'd lose his hold over his companions. That control had become very important to him. He'd had little say in his life until he'd met up with the river rats and the Forcer. Since then he'd felt like a man. And he played like a man. If sometimes somebody got hurt . . . well, that wasn't his fault. In big games somebody could get hurt. That's the way it was.

Even if his father was successful in getting him into

medical school, he would still need the Forcer as a source for his friends. He was more than sure that he'd passed the point of no return himself. It didn't matter. He'd keep his intake low. He'd managed to do that so far. At medical school he'd have a built-in source. Still, it would help if he knew who the Forcer was.

"What time do we get there, Robby?" Clyde asked.

"Nine-thirty. Everybody will've eaten and the dancing will have started. Most of them will have had a snootful. That's when we take her."

Divinity hadn't been so excited since her first prom. "I feel like a schoolgirl," she said to Jake as they drove to the country club.

"You look like a woman, though. I love that dress."

She smiled, looking down at the silk dress in soft coral hues that blended from dark to light. The short matching jacket was in the deepest tone. Draped like a sari, the dress showed every curve and was very flattering to her height and coloring. She wore a wool cape over it for warmth. "When my friend Destiny Smith worked in New York for a while, we patronized a neophyte designer on Third Avenue."

"Is Destiny's taste as good as yours?"

"Better. I think you'd like her. She's like you."

He sent her a questioning look.

"She's quietly good, just as you are." She watched him gulp. It was too dim in the Porsche for her to see if he was blushing. She guessed he was. She gazed out the windshield, sighing with contentment. How strange that she hadn't known real happiness until Jake had come into her life. It seemed as natural as breathing to love him.

He pulled into the parking lot that horseshoed around a sprawling white building. "The club. I've been coming here since I was a kid. It never looked better." He smiled at her. "I'm crazy about my date."

"Good. I kind of like you, too, big boy." She let her fingers feather over his cheek.

"Don't! I like it too much." He kissed her hand, then slid out of the Porsche. Going around to her side, he opened her door and smiled down at her. "Hi, beautiful. Ready to dance?"

"Yes." She put her hands in his and let him pull her to her feet. "This is a beautiful place. What do you think about it for a wedding reception?"

"Actually quite a few—What? What do you mean? Divinity, are you playing with me?" He stared down at her.

"You know I like to play with you. I thought you preferred privacy, though."

"Not funny. Did I misunderstand you?"

She shook her head. Then she laughed when he scooped her high in his arms and swung her around and around, his mouth pressed to her hair.

"Say it," he whispered.

"What?"

"You know, the words."

"Oh. The words." She savored the moment. "I love you, Jake Blessing, and I hope we have a family of boys just like you."

"Oh, God, don't wish for that. I was a terror." He kissed her long and hard.

"Not true. You were lonely and misunderstood. That won't happen again."

"It won't?"

"No."

"Great. That means you're committed to me, Brown. I won't let you call it back."

"I don't want to, Jake."

He kissed her, his mouth soft. "Soon?"

She nodded.

"I love it." He kissed her again, then hurried her into the building.

"Everyone in the county must be here," Divinity said after they'd checked their coats and walked into the dining area.

"The Hunt Club Ball is open to everyone. Most people around here come. It's a relaxing evening. The food is good, the music is country. What can I say?"

She smiled, sensing his happiness, knowing that Jake Blessing had had few really joyful times in his life. Yet he never hesitated to take trouble from the life of his friends. He was a very special man, and she thanked all the deities that he was hers.

He looked down at her. "What're you thinking?"

"That you're cute, and I'd better hurry up and snag you before someone else does."

"Not a chance." He leaned down to kiss her but someone called his name, forestalling him.

"What took you so long, Jake? We've been waiting." Darnell joined them, a beer in one hand, his arm around a shy young woman. "This is Cathy Page, Jake."

"I know her. How are you, Cathy?"

"Fine, Jake. That was sure something you did for Isaac. His folks live on a farm near ours, and he's such a good guy. Works hard."

"Thanks for saying that, Cathy. Don't forget to tell Isaac."

"I did." She turned to Divinity. "It was good of you, too, Ms. Brown." Cathy put out her hand. "Folks around here won't forget what you did."

Divinity shook her hand. "Thank you. Isaac is a fine person."

"The best. My father says nobody farms better than the Meistersaengers. He's good friends with Ephraim, Isaac's father."

"They're good people," Divinity agreed. When she turned around, she blinked. A large group of people faced her. Perplexed, she smiled. They smiled back.

One older man stepped forward. "We just wanted to tell you we thought you did a great job, Ms. Brown. I'm Hillyard Weems. Penny Elgin-Brown was the daughter of a good friend of mine. My wife and I doted on Penny." He looked downhearted. "She was like a daughter. We just knew Isaac wouldn't have hurt her." He frowned. "Wish we knew who did. Awful thing. Shouldn't have happened."

Others pressed forward, shaking her hand. Divinity was warmed by their praise and good wishes. When she looked around for Jake, she saw him leaning against the wall, watching her, smiling. You won't always take the backseat, Jake Blessing, she thought. She wouldn't let him.

After she'd spoken to a conga line of people, she felt a hand at her back. She knew that touch and leaned back.

"Sorry, folks," Jake said. "We came to dance."

Everyone laughed and moved back, forming a corridor of smiling faces that led to the dance floor.

Divinity looked up at Jake as they slow danced. "Don't you ever take any credit for the good you do?"

"I take credit for a lot of things."

"Stop being embarrassed." She grinned at him. "And you're hedging. You freight a good share of this county with jobs, low rent, cash in hand. Admit you're a softy."

"I do everyday stuff, not miracles like you." He leaned down and kissed her. "I have Grandmother's ring in my pocket. Would you let me announce our engagement?"

"Here? Tonight?"

He nodded.

"Well, I guess you could, but—"

"Don't change your mind." He stopped in the middle of the dance floor, lifted her hand, and slid the ring on her third finger. "Almost a perfect fit. Maybe I could have it sized down a hair."

Divinity shook her head. "Don't change anything. I'd rather put a guard on it." She looked up at him, feeling teary. "It's beautiful. I never hoped to wear anything so lovely. Emeralds are very special."

"They suit you."

She smiled, then lost her breath when he kissed her. Through the thundering in her ears she heard the sound of laughter and muted applause.

Jake lifted his head, grinning. "She's going to marry me," he announced.

Congratulations were offered as they were deluged from all sides with best wishes, hearty handshakes, even kisses.

When they were dancing again, Divinity cuddled against him, murmuring.

He bent his head to hers. "What did you say?"

"I said I got the best of the county, not the ne'er-do-well."

He stared down at her for a long moment. "You keep saying those wonderful things to me and we'll have to get married very soon."

"Sounds good."

They smiled at each other, and Divinity knew nothing could be more wonderful. The world was in place at last. She was Jake's. He was hers. Isaac's case had not gone to trial, and justice had triumphed. If there was the glitch of not knowing who the murderer was, that could come in time. The police were not about to let go of a capital murder case. Right now there was nothing to do but celebrate.

They were enjoying some of the local wine, trying to get cool after dancing several dances in a row, when another couple greeted them.

"Aaron! Dynasty!" Jake said, shaking Aaron's hand. "How are you? I'm engaged to Divinity."

Dynasty grabbed Divinity, hugging her and laughing. "I take full credit for this."

"And you should," Divinity whispered. "He's wonderful."

"I think so too."

Divinity stared at the arresting couple facing them. Both were tall, he with dark hair, she with red. They stood close to each other, seeming to be joined by an invisible thread. They'd earned their happiness the hard way, courage and love making them the strong duo they were. "After all you two have been through," Divinity said, "I thought you'd be down with your precious horses in Kentucky."

Dynasty grinned. "We had to be here for this. The Hunt Club Ball is a biggie in Yokapa County." She picked up Divinity's left hand. "Wait until Dorothy hears about this." She stretched on tiptoe, looking around. "She's here someplace. C'mon, you two, we have to find her."

"First I have to find the ladies' room," Divinity said.

Jake came up behind her, kissing her neck. "Hurry back."

"I will."

Divinity was surprised she didn't have a long wait in the ladies' room. When she came out of one of the cubicles, she was alone. She was leaning over the sink, applying a light lip gloss when a face appeared over her shoulder. "What are you—?" She whirled, putting her hands up when she saw Robby Cranston lift his fist.

The blow stunned her, but didn't knock her out.

Confused, she tried to pull herself together, keeping her eyes down, but not closing them all the way. How had Robby Cranston and another man gotten into the ladies' room? When he went to smack her again, she sagged and drove her fist into his groin.

His yowl gave her short triumph. She was smacked from behind and sank down, barely conscious. Hauled to the door, she tried to yell, but couldn't.

"We go out the same way we came in," Robby said. She was vaguely aware that she was being dragged down a dimly lit hallway, away from the noise and lights in the dining area. "I'll bet not five people know this door goes to the outside. It's a good thing you worked here once, Dilly."

"Yeah, yeah. Never mind the talk. Let's get out of here."

Divinity managed to open her mouth. Nothing exited but a groan.

"Should we gag her?"

"Naw. Who would hear her?"

"Right."

Divinity kept her body limp so they had to half drag, half carry her, slowing them up a bit. She tried to gather her scattered wits. Think! Think!

Jake kept looking over everybody's head.

"You're not listening, Junior."

"What? Oh, sure I am, Dorothy."

"What's wrong, son? You worried?"

Jake looked at the burly farmer who was as tall as

Jake himself and almost half again as wide. Pepper Lally was a shrewd, softhearted man who doted on his wife. "She's been in there too long." Even as he said the words, Jake was striding across the dance floor. He sensed that Pepper and Aaron were right behind him.

"Hey, Jake, what's up?" Darnell asked, then hopped behind Pepper. "He looks mad enough to chew stone. What's wrong with him, Pepper?"

"Worried," said the taciturn farmer.

"Uh-oh. I'll watch his back."

"Fine."

When Jake threw open the door to the ladies' room, there were some protests and one or two yelps. "Where's Divinity?"

"She's not here, Jake," Cathy Page said. "She wasn't here when I came in. Did you see her, Linnie?"

Jake didn't wait for an answer. "She's in trouble. We've got to find her."

Aaron grabbed Jake's arm. "I'll go out the back."

Jake nodded, then raced through the building and crashed through the front door. He heard her then.

"Jake! Jake!"

Heart in his mouth he raced across the parking lot barely noticing the thudding feet behind him. "I'm coming, Divinity," he shouted. Where was she? He scanned the parking lot, the putting greens, and the practice driving range.

Then he spotted them, three people struggling among a cluster of vans and trucks at the far edge of the parking lot. The engine on one van roared. Driven mad with fear, he raced toward the van.

A rock flew past his shoulder, smashing the van's windshield. Robby Cranston turned as Jake was almost on him. He pulled out a gun as Dilly tried to force a struggling Divinity into the van.

Desperate when she saw the gun aimed at Jake, Divinity threw out her leg as hard as she could, catching Robby once more in the groin. He bent over, groaning, giving Jake time.

He was on Cranston in seconds, throwing him to the ground. He wrestled Divinity away from Pilato, ducking a blow from the other man.

"Darling," he breathed, then set her aside and wheeled on the still crouching Robby Cranston. "I'm going to maim you, Cranston!"

"Get him!" Robby screamed. "Get him! Kill him!"

Dilly Pilato grabbed his gun from the front of the van.

A growling Pepper was there, hooking him around the waist and tossing him like a piece of firewood into the side of the van.

A dozen of Robby's cohorts poured from other vehicles, running into a horde of angry shouting men dressed in their best. It was a cacophonous brouhaha, everyone punching, shoving, bashing.

Jake kept Divinity behind him, swinging at Robby as he came off the ground, gun in hand.

"Get him, Pepper," Dorothy yelled, then swung her fist as one of Robby's buddies tried to get past her.

Divinity couldn't believe her eyes at the total melee. Most of the guests and workers at the ball had spilled into the parking lot. Some had taken sides, others cheered or booed the battlers, the mob circling the entire parking lot. Someone raced up behind Jake, and Divinity screeched, throwing herself at him, fists and feet flying. He backed off, then came at her again. Aaron whisked him off her and dispatched him with a punch in the stomach. He went down, sobbing for breath.

Divinity looked around. Dynasty and Dorothy were in the thick of it, shouting and swinging. Cathy was there, behind Darnell. Linnie smacked someone who'd taken a swing at Lithcomb.

"Now, honey, you stay back," Lithcomb told her, catching a blow on the head. Glowering, he turned around, grabbed the culprit by the seat of the pants and the neck of his shirt, and heaved. There was a distinct thud when he hit the ground. He didn't move.

Divinity tried to maneuver around Jake so she could help. He wouldn't let her. It delighted her when he cracked Robby in the jaw. She cheered.

Then police cars roared into the parking lot, sirens screaming and strobes flashing. In an instant the battle was over. The sudden silence was unnerving. When Robby moved to hop into the nearest truck, a well-muscled deputy yanked him back.

"What the hell's goin' on?" the sheriff growled.

A dozen people started speaking at once. The sheriff shouted them all to silence. Divinity stepped forward.

"I'd like to press charges against Robby Cranston and these two men." She pointed to Dilly Pilato and

Gil Pierce, who'd been behind the wheel of the van. "They tried to kidnap me."

Voices rose in outrage and denial as the sheriff ordered the three men handcuffed.

"Arrest her, Sheriff," Robby shouted. "She attacked *me!*"

"In the ladies' room? What were you doing there?" Divinity used her best courtroom voice.

"None of your business. I want a lawyer and my father."

"So that's why he wasn't here tonight. He colluded with you to perpetrate this crime?"

At Divinity's question the sheriff covered his eyes, muttering, "There goes my pension."

"No!" Robby shouted. "I want a lawyer."

"Don't forget to read him his rights, Sheriff, and the rest of his buddies too," Divinity said. "I don't want any technicalities getting in the way of the charges I'm going to make."

Robby was still asking for a lawyer as he and his friends were put into the squad cars.

As the place quieted, people looked down at themselves, examining torn and soiled clothing, muttering to one another.

Divinity looked from Jake to Aaron and Dynasty, to Pepper and Dorothy, and the others who'd come to her rescue. "I don't know how to thank you."

"Thank Jake, Ms. Brown," Darnell said, rubbing his jaw. "That sucker Dilly Pilato caught me."

"You did fine, Darnell." Cathy hugged him.

"I do thank Jake," Divinity whispered, turning in

his arms. She looked up at him, touching the puffiness under his eye. "You might have a shiner."

"It was worth ten broken bones."

"He was worried about you," Pepper said. "You were gone too long. He tore right into the ladies' room. When you weren't there, he tore out here. Madder'n hell he was." He looked down at his wife. "Pardon the language, sugar plum."

Dorothy tapped him on the cheek. "Don't be silly."

"Why did they do it, Jake?" Aaron asked, his arm around his wife.

"I don't know," Jake said through his teeth. "I'd heard Robby was damned mad that Isaac got off."

"You think he'd go after her 'cause of that?" Darnell winced when Cathy put an ice cube on his jaw she'd taken from a passing waiter.

Aaron nodded. "He could, especially if he was worried. Isaac's innocence would turn the limelight on him as the possible perpetrator. Right?"

Jake nodded. "I'm going to talk to LeRoy Wilkins again." LeRoy had been sleeping when he and Divinity had gone to the hospital earlier that day. He'd suffered a severe concussion, and the doctors wanted him disturbed as little as possible.

"I want to dance," Dorothy said. "Pepper, straighten your collar."

"Can't, m'love. It's torn."

"Oh, well, then leave it alone. I still want to dance. Come along and wash your hands first, and we'll have a cold beer."

Divinity chuckled. "She's something," she said to Jake. "No wonder you're scared of her."

"I'm not," Jake said.

"You are so," Pepper called back.

Everyone around them laughed, and Divinity heard several people say it was the best Hunt Club Ball ever.

That night as Divinity showered before going to bed, she wrestled with the fear rising in her. It had been growing since Robby had entered the rest room and accosted her, and hadn't stopped yet.

"It's over," Jake said, getting into the shower stall with her. "You're safe now."

"You read my mind?"

"It would be unnatural if you were able to just forget about what happened." He enfolded her in his arms. "I almost went out of my mind when I couldn't find you."

"You went into the ladies' room." She hiccuped a laugh against his chest.

"I would've gone to Hell."

She looked up at him. "I would have wanted you to do that." She tried to keep the tremor from her voice and failed.

"That son of a bitch frightened you," Jake said harshly.

She nodded. "I knew I couldn't let them put me in that van."

"I'm surprised they didn't gag you."

"They thought I was out cold. He hit me when we

were in the ladies' room and figured I was still groggy." Jake stiffened against her, and she blinked at the string of curses whistling from his throat. "Don't. It doesn't matter."

"It does. Cranston's going to jail. If his father tries to intervene, he can join his son in a cell." He looked down at her, cupping her jaw. "No one, ever, is going to get away with hitting or hurting you."

His graven features were alien to her. The easygoing ne'er-do-well had disappeared. In his place was an implacable force, willing to wreak violence to protect her. "Jake?"

"Hmm?" He tightened his arms around her. "What is it, angel?"

She touched his face. "I was frightened tonight, but underneath the fear was a certainty you'd rescue me. You did. I don't want vengeance to mar what we have. It's so rare to have such beauty. Don't let Robby Cranston or anyone else destroy that."

He took a few deep breaths, then kissed her. "You're right. Just don't get too uptight if I don't let you out of my sight."

She chuckled. "I won't."

He touched the swelling in her cheek. "Maybe I'd better get you into bed. I should call the doctor too. You could have a concussion."

She shook her head, putting her fingers on his lips. "I'm fine. I'll put some ice on this, then we can go to bed and make love. I think we do that very well. What do you think?"

"I think we're experts." Jake tried to keep it light.

It seemed to be what she wanted. For himself, he couldn't bury all his fear. Robby had to answer some questions. Jake was certain it hadn't been a spur of the moment attack. It had been planned.

"Should we teach a class?"

"What?" he asked.

"You're not paying attention to me. I said, should we teach a class on great sex?"

"No. Just keep teaching me."

"I can do that."

"So can I." He was going to keep his eye on her. No matter what she said, he was going to move on the Cranstons. He'd get his father's firm to represent his complaints.

"You're wandering again."

"I just had a good idea."

"What?"

"Maybe we should move to Washington or New York City. You could practice there again. I could handle my business from there." He smiled down at her. "I like big cities."

She shook her head. "We're not running, Jake. I'll be fine because I have you."

"Right." He kissed her hard, fear running over him like an icy shower.

# TEN

"You ask why I'm upset, Sandy? You think I should be celebrating because they're getting married? My son was arrested because of them." Fuming, Elliot Cranston strode up and down the picnic area.

Sandy Garret held back a sigh. "No, but there's no need to work yourself into a lather. I can almost guarantee that if Robby is found guilty, his sentence will only be community service. He'll still go to medical school. Even if he has to do time—"

Cranston rounded on Sandy, fury on his features. "It's not right. Isaac should've been convicted. Maybe my son wouldn't have gone a little crazy if justice had been done."

"Look, Elliot, I didn't like the judgment any more than you did. I think they freed a guilty man. It's a done deal. Let's put it behind us."

Cranston turned a dull red. "I don't like a blot on my son's record."

Sandy inhaled, not reminding Cranston of Robby's

speeding tickets. "And I told you he shouldn't have tried to kidnap that—"

"Kidnap? That's a nasty word," Cranston interrupted.

Sandy shook his head. "Not my call. That was the judge's. Finucane can be very touchy about some things. That's one of them. Tell Robby his best bet is to keep a low profile, his mouth shut, and continue to protest that Miss Brown misunderstood his intention. That it was all a game."

Cranston's high color receded a bit. He nodded. "I'll tell him." Rubbing his forehead, he exhaled. "I'll be glad when he's off to medical school. He was accepted at the one on Grenada." His smile was fleeting. "Maybe once he's out of the country he'll stop messing up."

Cranston shook his head. "Robby talks like a wild man sometimes. Says he won't go down alone, won't take any more of the blame. He told me before he was allowed out on bail that if he ever went to prison, he'd talk to some people. They'd know how to handle anyone on the outside. I told him I didn't like that kind of talk. Not that I want him to take full blame for what happened at the club. Those so-called friends of his shouldn't have included him in their games."

Sandy's lips tightened. "Right. Just tell him to keep his mouth shut except to profess his innocence. He was playing a game. Nothing more."

Cranston nodded, then watched as Sandy walked away. "I'll see you at the club."

Garret waved without looking back.

———◆———◆———

Robby slipped out of the house after dinner and met Pauley at the foot of the back garden.

"You okay, Robby? You sure your father didn't see you?"

"I'm fine. Let's get out of here. I feel like I've been in a real prison since I've been home. My mother cries all the time, my father lectures. Jeez, it's hell."

"Yeah. My old man never cares where I am as long as I don't get in his way."

"Who needs 'em?" Robby rubbed his hands together, eager to get away from the house. "Let's get some good stuff, Pauley."

Pauley patted the cellular phone Robby had given him. "Suits me. I just got a call. The Forcer is going to meet us at the old cabin."

"No kidding. He's never gone there."

"He'll be there. He said he has some great stuff for us. We can party."

Robby laughed. "Sounds good." He poked his friend in the arm. "I met some cool dudes in jail. Let me tell you . . ."

All the way to the landing on the river, he expounded on how great his fellow prisoners were, how knowledgeable. "I learned a lot."

Pauley grimaced. "I wished I'd been in on the raid at the club."

"We should've gotten away with it too. That fancy lawyer deserved what we were going to give her."

"Yeah."

"And you should see the connections they have, Pauley," Robby said over the hood of his friend's truck. "Big time." Robby grinned when Pauley hooted.

They drove to the shabby landing on the Seneca River that they'd used for a meeting place from time to time. Pauley unlocked the door to a dilapidated cabin. Inside the place was dark and airless.

As Robby reached for the switch, someone spoke. "Don't turn on the light."

"Why? Who are—?" Pauley's question was interrupted by the gun that pumped two bullets into his heart. He dropped to the floor.

"Hey!"

"So long, Robby. You've become too much trouble."

Robby stared down at his dead friend, then instinctively turned on the light. Facing him was a man dressed in a black wet suit, a mask covering most of his face. The man aimed his gun at Robby, and Robby turned to run. His hand was on the door when two slugs caught him high in the back.

The black-garbed figure checked that they were dead, then looked around the place to see if there was anything that could link him to the two lying on the floor.

With everything clean and neat, the front door and all the windows locked, the shades pulled, he left by the back door, securing it and tossing the key into the river. He slipped into the water unseen, using his air tank and head beam to guide him underwater for the half mile downstream to where his car was hidden.

# ELEVEN

Divinity was still awed that the wedding had been put together in such a short time. It had only been a week since the Hunt Club Ball. Nothing had deterred Jake.

"We love each other," he'd told her. "There's no reason to wait."

He'd been making love to her at the time, so she hadn't been able to come up with a protest. Besides, she wanted it as much as he did. Now there were only a few hours to wait.

The wedding was going to be at The Arbor, so Dorothy had badgered Jake until he'd agreed to spend the night before the wedding at his town house on Seneca Lake. It wasn't a long drive back to The Arbor, but he'd have to allow himself at least forty-five minutes so that he'd get there well before the ceremony started. He was itching to be there, to see her. He knew Dynasty, Aaron, Pepper, and Dorothy were arriving early to help Divinity, yet Jake didn't feel right.

If Lithcomb, Horace, and Milford hadn't spent the night at The Arbor, he wouldn't have left her at all.

Darnell and Butch, his two groomsmen, hadn't been much help. They'd come early that morning and kept popping into his bedroom to see how he was doing.

Jake turned around when Darnell stood in the doorway for the umpteenth time. "Now what?"

Darnell grinned. "Bride's on the phone. It's all right to talk to her, but you can't see—"

Jake didn't hear the rest. He ran to the bedside phone. "Hi. Don't back out. It won't do you any good. I'll follow you and camp on your doorstep."

Divinity laughed. "I'm not running. And you'd better not. I'll send the law."

"I was afraid of that. That's why I'll be there. When are Aaron and Dynasty due to arrive?"

"In about an hour. I have to get downstairs pretty soon. Harlan has fixed us a snack. He said food will settle me down. He doesn't want me to get queasy."

"Baloney. He doesn't want you to get cold feet. He can't wait to get me off his hands."

"How do you figure that if we'll be living here?"

"We will? Are you sure?"

"So sure that I might just run against Sanford S. Garret for district attorney."

"And you'd whup his butt too."

"I should go. I just wanted to say I love you."

"I love you, too, Divinity, more than my life."

"Hurry over here so I can snare you."

His laugh was husky. "On my way."

When he replaced the receiver, Darnell was still there. Jake scowled at him. "What?"

"You sure are hung up on her, boss."

Jake's scowl turned to a grin. "I am."


The house had a hollow sound when Divinity went downstairs. She was going to talk to Harlan about not making too much of a spread. She could manage something light, nothing more. Soon she'd be married to Jake, right there at The Arbor. It made her smile when she recalled how he'd balked at having to sleep at his town house instead of with her in the big bed in the master suite.

"Dynasty and Dorothy say it's traditional," she'd told him.

"I'm not marrying Dynasty or Dorothy."

His disgruntled tone had had her laughing. "You're cute when you pout."

"I'm not pouting, I'm flaming mad that I'm not sleeping with you tonight."

"You'll get over it." She had thrown her arms around his neck. "After tomorrow we'll be sharing the same bed for—"

"Ever," he'd said.

Sighing, she reached the bottom of the stairs. She glanced down the hall toward the kitchen, reminding herself she wanted to talk to Harlan. Then she looked around. Where were Lithcomb, Horace and . . . what was the other brother's name? No matter. Now, what was she going to do? The kitchen. Something turned her away, though, drawing her to the library. She pushed open the door, automatically shutting it behind her.

The desk was neat. She had put most of her research on Elmira Prison away. Now that Isaac's case was done, she might get back to it. She blinked when she noted the open book on the desk. It was the one she'd been reading the day she met Jake. Again it was open to the page with Mary Surratt's name. The name seemed to be magnified. It startled her when she looked up and the ghost was not where she usually stood, but behind the desk, her hand seeming to rest on the page, on the name. Surratt!

"What? What are you trying to tell me?"

The spirit looked at her fully for the first time. Her mouth formed one word. Danger!

Divinity's lips went slack with surprise. "What danger? Tell me."

"Do you always talk to the wall?"

She spun around. "What are you doing here?"

"I guess you didn't hear me come in. I spoke but you were busy talking to yourself."

She looked beyond him. "Where are—?"

"If you're asking about your guards, I think they're indisposed." He smiled.

"What do you mean?"

"It would be a waste of time looking for them or Harlan. They're not dead, but they won't feel very good when they wake up." He lifted his hand and put a strange-looking gun on the chair. "Tranquilizer gun. Quick. Easy."

Staring at him, Divinity felt surrounded by the danger the apparition had warned her of. She moved. So did he. Trapped. She tried to stall. "Ah, did you come in just now?"

"Yes."

"Strange. I didn't hear the door squeak. It usually does."

"Not this time."

She put her hand behind her, feeling on the desk for her letter opener. "What can I do for you, Garret?"

"You're stalling."

"Why would I do that?"

"You suspect something."

"What would I suspect, Mr. Garret? Or perhaps I could call you Sanford. Sanford S. Garret. What does the S stand for?"

"Certainly you can do better than that, Divinity. Very poor stalling tactics."

"Just because I'm interested in your middle name? Would it happen to be Surratt?" His arrested expression, the narrowing of his eyes, told her she'd hit the mark. That's what the spirit was trying to tell her? That the Surratt wasn't Mary, but Sanford. Divinity's mind computed with lightning speed, but she could hardly accept what it was telling her. Sanford Surratt Garret was a killer.

"Answer me."

She looked back at Garret. "What? I was thinking about Harlan. He should be in here any moment."

"I told you he's indisposed."

His smirk congealed her blood. "What have you done? Have you hurt him? Lithcomb—"

"They'll be out for a long time."

Caution kept her quiet, her mind tumbling over alternatives, none of which seemed feasible.

He inclined his head. "Ahh, the clever barrister has drawn some conclusions. What else do you think you know?"

She was walking a tightrope. It wasn't smart to show her hand. Neither was it wise to anger him by not answering. "Are you also called the Forcer?"

His eyebrows went up. "More informed than I thought."

He couldn't afford to let her live. She knew that, but she wasn't going to go down without some sort of fight. Oh dear Lord, her wedding day. What would Jake think?

When the telephone rang, they both looked at it.

# TWELVE

The phone rang as Jake was trying to knot the tie he'd chosen to go with his gray silk suit. They'd decided on a dressy informality. He grinned at his mirror image. What did he care? He'd marry Divinity in the buff on Fifth Avenue in the middle of Manhattan if she wanted it. He loved her and needed her more than he needed to breathe. Glancing at his watch, he started. He had less time than he figured. Too much daydreaming. He'd be damned if he'd be late for the wedding. He'd arranged a limo for Butch, Darnell, and himself. He grabbed the phone on the third ring. "Yeah?"

"Jake, it's Horace."

"Are you at The Arbor?"

"Lithcomb and Milford are there. I'm at the office. I'm going right back."

Something in his tone alerted Jake. "What's wrong?"

Horace cleared his throat. "Tell you the truth, I

haven't spoken to my brothers this morning. They didn't answer the phone, neither did Harlan. Now, don't get excited. They could be outside shoveling the driveway or stringing up crepe paper or something."

"Don't Lithcomb and Milford have beepers?"

"Sure. They don't go anywhere . . . Jake! Are you there?"

"Yeah. Call the sheriff. Tell him to get to The Arbor. And get the helicopter over here. Tell Willie I need her yesterday."

"Done. Jake, you don't think—?"

"Get on it." Jake broke the connection.

Throwing off the silk suit, he grabbed for jeans, a sweatshirt, and an old jacket. He changed out of the Gucci's into running shoes. At the last minute he paused, then slammed open a drawer and pulled out a thirty-eight. He loaded it, snapped it shut, and jammed it into the waistband of his jeans. Running down the stairs, he met Darnell and Butch. He told them there was trouble at The Arbor and to take the limo over there.

Sprinting out the front door to the expanse of lawn fronting on the lake, he looked skyward. The helicopter was coming right down Seneca Lake, dead on him. "I love you, Willie girl."

Even as she landed he was running toward her. "Fast as you can to The Arbor, Willie," he said as he climbed in.

"Going to tell me why, Jake? Horace is in an awful swivet. Same thing?"

At his sharp nod, she jammed the stick and they

accelerated. She maneuvered the bird as though it were a bicycle, getting them aloft fast. Instead of banking toward the shoreline of Seneca Lake, which was the usual route, she headed across it, full throttle. "I tried to call my other brothers at The Arbor. No answer. What's up, Jake?"

"I wish I knew. Divinity's in trouble, Willie. I can feel it."

Willie leaned over the controls, talking into the radio, then looked at Jake. "We'll beat the cops there. What do you want me to do?"

"Land me as close as you can without going on the property. I'll go in through the wine cellar."

Willie's smile was hard. "I've got my gun, Jake."

"I can't risk Divinity." He looked down at the farms that squared over the fields between the two largest Finger Lakes. "You'll have to set me down quite a ways from the place, Willie, because—"

"No, I won't." She grabbed her radio. "This'll cost you, Jake."

"Do it."

She spoke into the radio. A few minutes later they were in sight of Cayuga Lake. She pointed. "There's The Arbor, Jake. Looks pretty, doesn't it?"

He didn't answer. All at once two biplanes went past, buzzing them, then the mansion. He looked at Willie. "Good diversion."

"Those boys can fly, Jake. And they know what to do."

She circled down just beyond the old cemetery.

"There you are, Jake. I'll keep the engine off until I get a signal from you."

"Don't. Get out of here, Willie. I don't know what's in there, or what's wrong."

"I'm not bugging out, Jake. You should know better than to ask me."

Her words were lost on him. As soon as the copter hovered for landing, he was out and running.

"I think this has gone on long enough, Divinity. No more talking about the case, about me and what I do. Time to finish this." He glanced at his watch, his smile acidic. "You've managed to use up fifteen minutes." He pulled a gun from his pocket, brandishing it. "Noisy, but effective."

"I—" Before she could answer a plane roared over the house, circled, and came around again.

Garret looked out the window at the two biplanes that winged up, down and across the lake and back again. "I didn't know there was an air show today."

Divinity didn't even follow his glance. She was more concerned about finding the letter opener on her desk and getting it into her hand. She'd just grabbed it when he glanced at her. "Do you have anyone with you?" she asked.

His sudden laugh shook her. She licked her lips. "No one knew who you were, did they?"

He shook his head, grinning. "You mean among the river rats? Fine folks for fun and games, but not the type you'd want your name linked with, Divinity." He frowned. "You're hedging again. And you still haven't told me how you knew my middle name. Few people do." His frown deepened. "In fact, I'd be surprised if anybody in this county knew what it was. Have you been investigating me?"

"Yes." Divinity took a gamble that he'd want to know what she knew. "You made your case too personal, Garret. Why hate Isaac? He's no threat to you."

"Maybe I was just settling an old score. His father tongue-lashed me when he found me on his farm, running his milk cows. The old man deserved to squirm when his son was on the block."

"That's it?"

Dull red scored his face. "I worked as a part-time carpenter when I was in college. Too many times an Amish screwed me out of a job. I needed the money."

"So did they, I'm sure. Maybe the better craftsman got the job." She was taking a big risk jabbing at him. Who knew what he would do? He took umbrage at something that had happened years ago and attempted optimum revenge. Her only chance was to disarm him in some way, evening the odds.

His face contorted. "And what do you think you know?"

"That you've been masquerading for years behind this role of the noble district attorney while playing your nasty little games with innocent young women."

He glared at her. "You're a busybody, Divinity Brown, and a nuisance. I might have let you live if Isaac Meistersaenger had been convicted as he should've been." His eyes seemed to glaze. "I wouldn't like it if anyone connected me with Cranston and that crowd."

"You might have to kill him too. Robby tends to run off at the mouth." The strange twist to his lips chilled her blood. She had the distinct sensation that the matter had been handled.

"I take care of problems as they arise." His mouth tightened. "Isaac should've been convicted."

"He was innocent. You wanted him to pay for your nastiness. Only a coward wants an innocent man to pay for his crimes. You've hurt too many women." She knew she'd made a big mistake as the words left her mouth.

His face curled into a mask of hate. "So you figured there was more than one whore, did you?"

"Yes," she whispered.

"You weren't that smart, Divinity. I used the second floor of The Arbor barn to store the body parts until I could bury Penny and her kid. That's the last place anyone would look. I knew from overhearing Harlan that the area was rarely used." He bared his teeth. "She might've bluffed Cranston because she was smart. Then, again, she didn't know she'd have to face me. I won't tolerate cheap whores interfering with me."

"Why?"

"I like games. They keep you sharp for the big encounters. Those females weren't important to anyone, and they provided the outlet I need from time to time." He lifted a shoulder in dismissal. "They served a purpose." His smile had all the warmth of a striking rattler. "Since you will die, I'll tell you something. Penny Elgin-Brown was the most fun. She fought." He jerked his head toward the window. "She's buried in the old cemetery back there, her parts, that is. No one will ever find her."

Divinity swallowed bile, fear, and rage.

A movement caught her eye, but she didn't look. He was too perceptive. He'd notice. "How many were there?"

He brought the gun up as though he were about to shake hands with her. "The three you mentioned in the hearing. Some others." His smile widened. "You have to die."

Divinity gulped. "Do you think you can get away with this? People will be arriving soon, and—"

"Not for at least thirty minutes. I can—"

Garret almost turned in time, his reflexes carrying him around as Jake hit him. The gun went off, firing into the ceiling.

Divinity screamed.

The two men rolled on to the floor, wrestling for the gun. Garret held on to it even as he grappled with Jake, both men grunting with effort.

Divinity glanced around the room, desperately searching for a weapon, something larger and potentially more damaging than the letter opener. She stumbled toward the fireplace and seized the poker. As she turned, she saw the ghost. It was staring at Jake and Garret.

"Help him," Divinity said.

Divinity charged at the two men, swinging the poker. Supreme luck was on her side as she struck a glancing blow at Garret's hand and the gun flew. Then she was knocked to the floor. On hands and knees she went after the gun.

"No, you don't," Garret growled, then he was atop her, trying to wrest the gun from her. When he screamed, Divinity stopped struggling and looked over her shoulder.

Jake was pulling himself erect, his face bloodied. They both stared at Garret as he rose to his feet, howling, then left the door at a dead run.

Jake pulled Divinity off the floor. "Are you all right, darling?"

She nodded.

"Stay here. I'm going after him."

She shook her head, fear closing her throat.

"Don't worry. I'll be right back. We're getting married today."

She nodded. "Jake . . . Jake, I love you. Be careful."

"I love you, and I will."

He was gone before she could say any more. She called 911, somehow got her message across, and slammed down the phone. She had to find Jake. No matter what he said, she could help him. Garret was a despicable man. He'd stop at nothing. She couldn't let him hurt Jake. She picked up the gun from the floor.

Jake tracked him as he would have tracked game. Though he'd given up hunting years ago, he'd not lost his ability to search and find.

He followed Garret's trail to the cemetery. There he paused, hearing a struggle, but seeing nothing. Then he spotted Garret. Stunned, he could only stare. Garret was wrestling with a ghost. No, a group of wraiths had surrounded him. Jake swallowed, not sure what he should do. Garret didn't have a weapon, but he was fighting mightily with the spirits surrounding him. Of course, what good would a weapon have done him?

Hearing someone staggering through the knee-high snow behind him, he turned and saw Divinity topping the ridge. He went to her and pulled her into his arms, then pointed to Garret.

In silence they watched the struggling man as the spirits urged him to the far end of the cemetery. Jake sucked in his breath, knowing that beyond the cemetery was a cliff. Garret yelled and cursed as the ghosts maneuvered him to the cliff edge. He lost his footing and fell, dropping from their sight, though they heard his screams stringing out behind him, then a sickening thud, then silence.

Shaken, Jake and Divinity clung to each other. Neither spoke as one of the ghosts turned and drifted toward them. She smiled and mouthed a thank-you. Then she was gone.

Jake and Divinity teetered between credulity and disbelief.

"I can hardly believe it happened, Jake."

"It did, darling."

"I never expected a ghost from the past to help me because I was writing about the Civil War."

"Darling, maybe she was from your family, but she wasn't from the Civil War. I recognized the one who came toward us. That was Penny Elgin-Brown."

Tears started from Divinity's eyes. She looked up at the man she loved. "Then the others must've been—"

"The other girls he killed."

"They saved both of us. Penny tried to tell me from the beginning."

Jake nodded. "Maybe she can rest now." He put his arm around her and kissed her hair. "She was a brave woman, and she knew you were, too, and would understand her pain. That's why she came to you." When he saw the tears in her eyes, he hugged her. "You're the best, lady, and I'm glad you're mine." He sighed. "And I'm glad Garret can't hurt any more women."

"Penny's buried here, Jake. I think we should leave her here, maybe even erect a memorial for her and the others."

"We can do that. Come on, lady. I want to get married."

"So do I, Jake, so do I."

She looked over her shoulder at where the ghosts had been, smiling. "One day I'm going to tell our children about the brave women who helped us."

"We'll both tell them," Jake said, tightening his hold.

Arms around each other they left the cemetery.

Neither noticed the cluster of wraiths when they reappeared and how they smiled after them. One held a child. Then each of the spirits looked toward the cliff, disappearing one by one into the light mist coming off the lake.

# THE EDITORS' CORNER

Along with May flowers come four fabulous LOVESWEPTs that will dazzle you with humor, excitement, and, above all, love. Touching, tender, packed with emotion and wonderfully happy endings, our four upcoming romances are real treasures.

Starting the lineup is the innovative Ruth Owen with **AND BABIES MAKE FOUR,** LOVESWEPT #786. Naked to the waist, his jeans molded to his thighs like a second skin, Sam Donovan looks like trouble—untamed and shameless! Dr. Noel Revere hadn't expected her guide to the island's sacred places to be so uncivilized, but this rebel sets her blood on fire and stirs her insides like a runaway hurricane. Can they survive a journey into the jungle shared by two matchmaking computers with mating on their minds? Once again,

Ruth Owen delivers an exotic adventure that is both wildly sexy and wickedly funny!

In her enchanting debut novel, **KISS AND TELL**, LOVESWEPT #787, Suzanne Brockmann adds a dash of mystery to a favorite romantic fantasy. When Dr. Marshall Devlin spots Leila Hunt alone on the dance floor, he yearns to charm the violet-eyed Cinderella into his arms, but how can he court the lady when they fight over everything, and always have? Then the clock strikes twelve and Leila is possessed by the passion of a familiar stranger. He captures her lips—and her soul—in a moment of magic, but can she learn to love the man behind the mask?

From award-winning author Terry Lawrence comes **FUGITIVE FATHER**, LOVESWEPT #788. A single light burned in the window of the isolated lakeside cottage, but Ben Renfield wondered which was the greater risk—hiding in the woods to evade his pursuers or seeking refuge with a beautiful stranger! Touched by his need, tempted by her own, Bridget Bernard trades precious solitude for perilous intimacy . . . and feels her own walls begin to crack. Can rescuing a lonely warrior transform her own destiny? Terry Lawrence blends simmering suspense and stunning sensuality in a tale that explores the tender mysteries of the human heart.

Finally, there's **STILL MR. & MRS.**, LOVESWEPT #789, by talented newcomer Patricia Olney. Two years before, they'd embraced in a heated moment, courted in one sultry afternoon, and wed in a reckless promise to cherish forever. Now Gabriel and Rebecca Stewart are days from the heart-breaking end of a dream! When a business crisis demands a last-minute lover's charade, Gabe offers Reb anything she wants—but will their seductive game of "let's pretend" ignite flames of dangerous desire? In this delicious story of second chances, Patricia Olney makes us believe in the enduring miracle of love.

Happy reading!

With warmest wishes,

Beth de Guzman

Senior Editor

Shauna Summers

Editor

P.S. Watch for these Bantam women's fiction titles coming in April: From the *New York Times* bestselling author Betina Krahn comes another blockbuster romance filled with her patented brand of love and laughter in **THE UNLIKELY ANGEL**. Also welcome nationally bestselling author Iris Johansen in her hardcover debut of **THE UGLY DUCKLING**, a tale of contemporary romantic suspense! **DANGEROUS TO HOLD** by Elizabeth Thornton is filled with her trademark passion and suspense, and **THE REBEL AND THE REDCOAT** by Karyn

Monk promises a scorching tale of passion set against the dramatic backdrop of the American Revolution! Be sure to see next month's LOVE-SWEPTs for a preview of these exceptional novels. And immediately following this page, preview the Bantam women's fiction titles on sale now!

A tantalizing tale of a legendary knight and a headstrong lady whose daring quest for a mysterious crystal will draw them into a whirlwind of treachery—and desire.

From *New York Times* bestseller

# Amanda Quick

comes

# MYSTIQUE

*When the fearsome knight called Hugh the Relentless swept into Lingwood Manor like a storm, everyone cowered—except Lady Alice. Sharp-tongued and unrepentant, the flame-haired beauty believed Sir Hugh was not someone to dread but the fulfillment of her dreams. She knew he had come for the dazzling green crystal, knew he would be displeased to find that it was no longer in her possession. Yet Alice had a proposition for the dark and forbidding knight: In return for a dowry that would free Alice and her brother from their uncle's grasp, she would lend her powers of detection to his warrior's skills and together they would recover his treasured stone. But even as Hugh accepted her terms, he added a condition of his own: Lady Alice must agree to a temporary betrothal—one that would soon draw her deep into Hugh's great stone fortress, and into a battle that could threaten their lives . . . and their only chance at love.*

*From the winner of the* Romantic Times
*Storyteller of the Year Award comes*

# DIABLO
## by **Patricia Potter**

*Raised in a notorious outlaw hideout, Nicky Thompson learned to shoot fast, ride hard, and hold her own against killers and thieves. Yet nothing in her experience prepared her for the new brand of danger that just rode in. Ruggedly handsome, with an easy strength and a hint of deviltry in his smile, Diablo made Nicky's heart race not with fright but with a sizzling arousal. When she challenged him to taste her womanly charms, she didn't know he was a condemned convict who'd come to Sanctuary with one secret purpose—to destroy it in exchange for pardons for himself and a friend. Would a renegade hungry for freedom jeopardize his dangerous mission for a last chance at love?*

With a sigh of pure contentment, Kane relaxed in the big tin bathtub in an alcove off the barber's shop. One hand rubbed his newly shaved cheek. The barber had been good, the water hot. The shave had been sheer luxury, costing five times what it would have in any other town, but that didn't bother him. In truth, it amused him. He was spending Marshal Ben Masters's money.

He lit a long, thin cigar that he'd purchased, also at a rather high price. He supposed he was as close to heaven as he was apt to get. Sinking deeper into the water, he tried not to think beyond this immediate pleasure. But he couldn't forget his friend Davy. The leash, as Masters so coldly called it, pulled tight around his neck.

Reluctantly, he rose from the tub and pulled on the new clothes he'd purchased at the general store. Blue denim trousers, a dark blue shirt. A clean bandanna around his neck. The old one had been beyond redemption. He ran a comb through his freshly washed hair, trying to tame it, and regarded himself briefly in the mirror. The scar stood out. It was one of the few he'd earned honorably, but it was like a brand, forever identifying him as Diablo.

Hell, what difference did it make? He wasn't here to court. He was here to betray. He couldn't forget that. Not for a single moment.

With a snort of self-disgust, he left the room for the stable. He would explore the boundaries of Sanctuary, do a reconnaissance. He had experience at that. Lots of experience.

Nicky rode for an hour before she heard gunshots.

She headed toward the sound, knowing full well that a stray bullet could do as much damage as a directed one. Her brother Robin was crouching, a gunbelt wrapped around his lean waist, his hand on the grip of a six-shooter. In a quick movement, he pulled it from the holster and aimed at a target affixed to a tree. Then he saw Nicky.

The pride on his face faltered, and then he set his jaw rebelliously and fired. He missed.

Nicky turned her attention to the man next to him. Arrogance radiated from him as he leered at her. Her skin crawling, she rode over to them and addressed Cobb Yancy. "If my uncle knew about this, you would be out of Sanctuary faster than a bullet from that gun."

"That so, honey?" Yancy drawled. "Then he'd have to do something about your baby brother, wouldn't he?" He took the gun from Robin and stood there, letting it dangle from his fingers.

Nicky held out her hand. "Give me the gun."

"Why don't you take it from me?" Yancy's voice was low, inviting.

"You leave now, and I'll forget about this," she said.

"What if I don't want you to forget about it?" he asked, moving toward her horse. "The boy can take your horse back. You can ride with me." His hand was suddenly on the horse's halter.

"Robin can walk back," she said, trying to back Molly. Yancy's grasp, though, was too strong.

Yancy turned to Robin. "You do that, boy. Start walking."

Robin looked from Yancy to Nicky and back again, apprehension beginning to show in his face. "I'd rather ride back with you, Mr. Yancy."

The gun was suddenly pointed at Robin. "Do as I say. Your sister and I will be along later."

Nicky was stiff with anger and not a little fear. "My uncle will kill you," Nicky pointed out.

"He may try," Yancy said. "I've been wondering if he's as fast as everyone says."

Nicky knew then that Cobb Yancy had just been looking for an excuse to try her uncle. Had he scented weakness? Was he after Sanctuary?

She felt for the small derringer she'd tucked inside a pocket in her trousers. "Go on, Robin," she said. "I'll catch up to you."

Robin didn't move.

"Go," she ordered in a voice that had gone hard.

Softness didn't survive here, not in these mountains, not among these men.

Instead of obeying her, Robin lunged for the gun in Yancy's hand. It went off, and Robin went down. Nicky aimed her derringer directly at Yancy's heart and fired.

He looked stunned as the gun slipped from his fingers and he went down on his knees, then toppled over. Nicky dismounted and ran over to Robin. Blood was seeping from a wound in his shoulder.

She heard hoofbeats and grabbed the gun Yancy had been holding. It could be his brother coming.

But it wasn't. It was Diablo, looking very different than he had earlier. He reined in his horse at the sight of the gun aimed in his direction. His gaze moved from her to Robin to the body on the ground.

"Trouble?"

"Nothing I can't handle," Nicky said, keeping the gun pointed at him.

The side of his mouth turned up by the scar inched higher. "I see you can," he said, then studied Robin. "What about him?"

"My brother," she explained stiffly. "That polecat shot him."

"I think he needs some help."

"Not from you, mister," she said.

His brows knitted together, and he shifted in the saddle. Then ignoring the threat in her hand, he slid down from his horse and walked over to Robin, pulling the boy's shirt back to look at the wound.

Robin grimaced, then fixed his concentration on Diablo's scar. "You're that new one," he said. "Diablo."

Diablo nodded. "Some call me that. How in the hell did everyone around know I was coming?"

"There's not many secrets here," Robin said, but his voice was strained. He was obviously trying to be brave for the gunslinger. Nicky sighed. Hadn't he learned anything today?

Diablo studied the wound a moment, then took off his bandanna and gave it to Robin. "It's clean. Hold it to the wound to stop the bleeding."

He then went over to Cobb Yancy, checked for signs of life and found none. He treated death very casually, Nicky noticed. "He's dead, all right," Diablo said.

Before she could protest, he returned to Robin. He helped Robin shed his shirt, which he tore in two and made into a sling. When he was through, he offered a steadying arm to Robin.

"Don't," Nicky said sharply. "I'll help him."

"He's losing blood," Diablo said. "He could lose consciousness. You prepared to take his whole weight?"

Nicky studied her brother's face. It was pale, growing paler by the moment. "We'll send someone back for Yancy. He has a brother. It would be best not to meet him."

Diablo didn't ask any questions, she'd give him that. She looked down at her hands and noticed they were shaking. She'd never killed a man before.

Diablo's eyes seemed to stab through her, reading her thoughts. Then he was guiding Robin to Yancy's horse, practically lifting her brother onto the gelding. There was an easy strength about him, a confidence, that surprised Nicky. He'd looked so much the renegade loner that morning, yet here he'd taken charge automatically, as if he were used to leadership. Resentment mixed with gratitude.

She tucked the gun into the waist of her trousers

and mounted her mare. She kept seeing Yancy's surprised face as he went down. Her hands were shaking even more now. She'd killed a man. A man who had a very dangerous brother.

She had known this would happen one day. But nothing could have prepared her for the despair she felt at taking someone's life. She felt sick inside.

Diablo, who was riding ahead with Robin, looked back. He reined in his own horse until she was abreast of him, and she felt his watchful gaze settle on her. "Tell Yancy's brother I did it."

Nothing he could have said would have surprised her more.

"Why?"

"I can take care of myself."

He couldn't have insulted her more. "And what do you think *I* just did?"

"I think you just killed your first man, and you don't need another on your conscience. You certainly don't need it on your stomach. You look like you're going to upchuck."

She glared at him. "I'm fine."

"Good. Your brother isn't."

All of Nicky's attention went to Robin. He was swaying in his saddle. She moved her horse around to his side. "Just a few more minutes, Robin. Hold on."

"I'm sorry, Sis. I shouldn't have gone with . . . Cobb Yancy, but—"

"Hush," she said. "If you hadn't, Yancy would have found something else. He was after more than me."

But Robin wasn't listening. He was holding on to the saddle horn for dear life, and his face was a white mask now.

"Maybe I should ride ahead," she said. "Get some help."

"You got a doctor in this place?" Diablo asked.

"Not right now. But Andy—"

"Andy?"

"The blacksmith. He knows some medicine, and I can sew up a wound."

"Go on ahead and get him ready," Diablo ordered. "I'll get your brother there." He stopped his horse, slipped off, and then mounted behind Robin, holding him upright in the saddle.

Could she really trust Diablo that much? Dare she leave him alone with Robin?

"I'll take care of him," Diablo said, more gently this time.

Nicky finally nodded and spurred her mare into a gallop.

Wearing it was just asking for trouble

# THE BAD LUCK WEDDING DRESS

The most memorable Texas romance yet
from the uniquely talented

# Geralyn Dawson

"One of the best new authors to come along in
years—fresh, charming, and romantic!"
—*New York Times* bestselling author Jill Barnett

*They were calling it the Bad Luck Wedding Dress, and
Jenny Fortune knew that spelled trouble for her Fort
Worth dressmaking shop. Just because the Bailey girls had
met with one mishap or another after wearing Jenny's
loveliest creation, her clientele had begun to stay away in
droves. Yet Jenny was still betting she could turn her luck
around—by wearing the gown herself at her very own
wedding. There's just one hitch: first she has to find a
groom. . . .*

While people all over the world have strange ideas
about luck, Fort Worth, being a gambling town,
seemed to have stranger ideas than most. Folks here
made bets on everything, from the weather to the
length of the sermon at the Baptist church on Sunday.
Jenny theorized that this practice contributed to a
dedicated belief in the vagaries of luck, making it easy
for many to lay the blame for the Baileys' difficulties
on the dress.

Monique shrugged. "Well, I think you're wrong. Give it a try, dear. It's a perfect solution. And you needn't be overly concerned with your lack of a beau. Despite your father's influence, you are still my daughter. The slightest of efforts will offer you plenty of men from whom to choose. Now, I think you should start with this."

She pulled the pins from Jenny's chignon, fluffed out her wavy blond tresses, then pressed a kiss to her cheek. "I'm so glad I was able to help, dear. Now I'd best get back to the station. Keep me informed about the developments, and if you choose to follow my advice, be sure to telegraph me with the date of the wedding. I'll do my best to see that your father drags his nose from his studies long enough to attend."

"Wait, Monique," Jenny began. But the dressing-room curtains flapped in her mother's wake, and the front door's welcome bell tinkled before she could get out the words "I can't do these back buttons myself."

Wonderful. Simply wonderful. She closed her eyes and sighed. It'd be just her luck if not a single woman entered the shop this afternoon. "The Bad Luck Wedding Dress strikes again," she grumbled.

Of course she didn't believe it. Jenny didn't believe in luck, not to the extent many others did, anyway. People could be lucky, but not things. A dress could not be unlucky any more than a rabbit's foot could be lucky. "What's the saying?" she murmured aloud, eyeing her reflection in the mirror. "The rabbit's foot wasn't too lucky for the rabbit?"

Jenny set to work twisting and contorting her body, and eventually she managed all but two of the buttons. Grimacing, she gave the taffeta a jerk and felt the dress fall free even as she heard the buttons plunk against the floor.

While she gave little credit to luck, she did believe rather strongly in fate. As she stepped out of the wedding gown and donned her own dress, she considered the role fate had played in leading her to this moment. It was fate that she'd chosen to make Fort Worth her home. Fate that the Baileys had chosen her to make the dress. Fate that the brides had suffered accidents.

The shop's bell sounded. "*Now* someone comes," she whispered grumpily. "Not while I'm stuck in a five-hundred-dollar dress and needing assistance." She stooped to pick the buttons up off the floor and immediately felt contrite. She'd best be grateful for any customer, and besides, she welcomed the distraction from her troublesome thoughts.

Pasting a smile on her face, Jenny exited the dressing room and spied Mr. Trace McBride entering her shop.

He was dressed in work clothes—black frock jacket and black trousers, white shirt beneath a gold satin vest. He carried a black felt hat casually in his hand and raked a hand nervously through thick, dark hair.

Immediately, she ducked back behind the curtain.

*Oh, my.* Her heart began to pound. Why would the one man in Fort Worth, Texas, who stirred her imagination walk into her world at this particular moment?

She swallowed hard as she thought of her mother's advice. It was a crazy thought. Ridiculous.

But maybe, considering the stakes, it wouldn't hurt to explore the idea. Jenny had the sudden image of herself clothed in the Bad Luck Wedding Dress, standing beside Trace McBride, his three darling daughters looking on as she repeated vows to a preacher.

Her mouth went dry. Hadn't she sworn to fight for Fortune's Design? Wasn't she willing to do whatever it took to save her shop? If that meant marriage, well . . .

Wasn't it better to give up the dream of true love than the security of her independence?

Jenny stared at her reflection in the mirror. What would it hurt to explore her mother's idea? She wouldn't be committing to anything.

Jenny recalled the lessons she'd learned at Monique's knees. Flirtation. Seduction. That's how it was done. She took a deep breath. Was she sure about this? Could she go through with it? She *was* Monique Day's daughter. Surely that should count for something. She could do this.

Maybe.

Trace McBride. What did she really know about him? He was a businessman, saloon keeper, landlord, father. His smile made her warm inside and the musky, masculine scent of him haunted her mind. Once when he'd taken her arm in escort, she couldn't help but notice the steel of his muscles beneath the cover of his coat. His fingers would be rough against the softness of her skin. His kiss would be—

Jenny startled. Oh, bother. Had she lost her sense entirely?

Perhaps she had. She was seriously considering her mother's idea.

What was she thinking? He'd never noticed her before; what made her think he'd notice her now? What made her think he'd even consider such a fate as marriage?

Fate. There was that word again.

Was Trace McBride her fate? Could he save her from the rumor of the Bad Luck Wedding Dress? Could he help her save Fortune's Design?

She wouldn't know unless she did a little exploring. Was she brave enough, woman enough, to try?

She was Jenny Fortune. What more was there to say?

Taking a deep breath, Jenny pinched her cheeks, fluffed her honey-colored hair, and walked out into the shop.

# On sale in April:

**THE UGLY DUCKLING**
by Iris Johansen

**THE UNLIKELY ANGEL**
by Betina Krahn

**DANGEROUS TO HOLD**
by Elizabeth Thornton

**THE REBEL AND THE
REDCOAT**
by Karyn Monk

*To enter the sweepstakes outlined below, you must respond by the date specified and
follow all entry instructions published elsewhere in this offer.*

## DREAM COME TRUE SWEEPSTAKES

Sweepstakes begins 9/1/94, ends 1/15/96. To qualify for the Early Bird Prize, entry must be received by the
e specified elsewhere in this offer. Winners will be selected in random drawings on 2/29/96 by an indepen-
t judging organization whose decisions are final. Early Bird winner will be selected in a separate drawing
m among all qualifying entries.

Odds of winning determined by total number of entries received. Distribution not to exceed 300 million.

Estimated maximum retail value of prizes: Grand (1) $25,000 (cash alternative $20,000); First (1) $2,000;
ond (1) $750; Third (50) $75; Fourth (1,000) $50; Early Bird (1) $5,000. Total prize value: $86,500.

Automobile and travel trailer must be picked up at a local dealer; all other merchandise prizes will be
pped to winners. Awarding of any prize to a minor will require written permission of parent/guardian. If a
 prize is won by a minor, s/he must be accompanied by parent/legal guardian. Trip prizes subject to avail-
lity and must be completed within 12 months of date awarded. Blackout dates may apply. Early Bird trip is
 a space available basis and does not include port charges, gratuities, optional shore excursions and onboard
sonal purchases. Prizes are not transferable or redeemable for cash except as specified. No substitution for
zes except as necessary due to unavailability. Travel trailer and/or automobile license and registration fees
 winners' responsibility as are any other incidental expenses not specified herein.

Early Bird Prize may not be offered in some presentations of this sweepstakes. Grand through third prize
ners will have the option of selecting any prize offered at level won. All prizes will be awarded. Drawing will
held at 204 Center Square Road, Bridgeport, NJ 08014. Winners need not be present. For winners list (avail-
e in June, 1996), send a self-addressed, stamped envelope by 1/15/96 to: Dream Come True Winners, P.O.
 572, Gibbstown, NJ 08027.

## THE FOLLOWING APPLIES TO THE SWEEPSTAKES ABOVE:

No purchase necessary. No photocopied or mechanically reproduced entries will be accepted. Not responsi-
for lost, late, misdirected, damaged, incomplete, illegible, or postage-die mail. Entries become the property
sponsors and will not be returned.

Winner(s) will be notified by mail. Winner(s) may be required to sign and return an affidavit of eligibility/
:ase within 14 days of date on notification or an alternate may be selected. Except where prohibited by law, entry
stitutes permission to use of winners' names, hometowns, and likenesses for publicity without additional com-
sation. Void where prohibited or restricted. All federal, state, provincial, and local laws and regulations apply.

All prize values are in U.S. currency. Presentation of prizes may vary; values at a given prize level will be
oximately the same. All taxes are winners' responsibility.

Canadian residents, in order to win, must first correctly answer a time-limited skill testing question admin-
ered by mail. Any litigation regarding the conduct and awarding of a prize in this publicity contest by a resi-
t of the province of Quebec may be submitted to the Regie des loteries et courses du Quebec.

Sweepstakes is open to legal residents of the U.S., Canada, and Europe (in those areas where made avail-
e) who have received this offer.

Sweepstakes in sponsored by Ventura Associates, 1211 Avenue of the Americas, New York, NY 10036 and
sented by independent businesses. Employees of these, their advertising agencies and promotional compa-
s involved in this promotion, and their immediate families, agents, successors, and assignees shall be ineli-
le to participate in the promotion and shall not be eligible for any prizes covered herein.     SWP 3/95